Karen McCarthy was born [...]
mother and Jamaican fat[...]
publishing and the media fo[...]
of the critically acclaim[...]
Contemporary Black Women's Poetry (The Women's Press,
1998), nominated for Best Book in the EMMA Awards
2000, she has presented her work nationwide at venues
including the Poetry Society, the South Bank Centre and
at the international women's art festival in Slovenia as
part of the British Council's New British Writing
promotion. She runs workshops and surgeries on editing
skills for new and emerging authors and is also a reviewer
and writer herself.

Also edited by Karen McCarthy

Bittersweet:
Contemporary Black Women's Poetry

KIN

New Fiction by Black and Asian Women

Edited by

Karen McCarthy

First published by Serpent's Tail, 2003
4 Blackstock Mews, London N4 2BT
www.serpentstail.com

Library of Congress Catalog Card Number: 2003110079

British Library Cataloguing-in-Publication Data
A catalogue record for this book is available from the British Library.

ISBN 1 85242 852 X

Typeset in 11/15pt Berling by FiSH Books, London WC1
Printed and bound in Great Britain by Mackays of Chatham, Kent

ACKNOWLEDGEMENTS

With heartfelt thanks to my editor Charlotte Cole, who always had faith in me and the project. I'd also like to thank Pete Ayrton at Serpent's Tail for stepping into the breach so quickly and efficiently; Melanie Abrahams at renaissance one for her work on the live literature tour of the same name, and the Arts Council of England for funding it. I am particularly grateful to the London Arts Board for their generous assistance, without which this book would not have been possible. Last and by no means least, I would like to acknowledge and thank all the writers who submitted their work to *Kin*, as well as all the individuals and organisations that have supported this publication and helped spread the word about the book.

CONTENTS

INTRODUCTION

My father always told me, 'You must *know* who your family is!' I always thought this was a rather obvious comment, until one day, when I was fourteen, he appeared on the front doorstep, with a pleased-looking grin on his face and a slim, dark and handsome young man at his side. 'I've got someone I'd like you to meet,' he announced. I turned a violent shade of red, convinced of the very worst: he had decided to take matters into his own hands and set me up with a suitable boy. As it turned out, it was my older brother from Jamaica who had come to check out life in London before settling in New York. Clearly all this paternal advice had not been offered for sentimental reasons. Over the years, he always made sure that when one of my brothers from America, Jamaica or Sweden (another story altogether) came to visit, we were properly introduced.

I tell this story because what each of us conceives as family is inevitably unique. When I read Barbara A. Graham's powerful story 'Next of Kin' it resonated with me for days. It made me think about families and about the many secrets that every family holds – whether that family is of the supposedly standard 2.4 children or the three sisters, two brothers and a step-sibling variety. It made me think about what our understanding of family – or kin – is today, and it made me think about family as a larger, political construct, and how that relates to the black and Asian writers whose work is gathered together here.

What we understand from the word 'kin' stretches beyond the biological, in that it's not so much about who our relations and ancestors are, but what we do and how we feel about those who are close to us. Often, the people we dance, eat and sleep with and the friends we can trust and rely on are family too. Similarly, family can also be people with whom we share common aims and concerns, and, in the diasporan sense, a common history of exile or migration. Writers, too, can be part of a literary community – and though as individual family members they may have to compete for attention if they want to stand out from the crowd, the strength and collective knowledge of the clan is there to draw on, as and when they need it. This broader definition of the term stretches to the anthology itself, with the theme of kinship being more of a loose ribbon than a tight band: not all the stories concern blood relations, but all explore the complexities of our closest ties and friendships. With this in mind, it was important to me that the stories fitted together well, so the collection itself could also be something of a family.

That said, I did not start by having a set idea of the kind of stories that would appear in *Kin*. I wanted the compass of inclusion to be as wide as possible – to reflect the diverse nature of what constitutes being black and/or Asian in Britain today. The world we now inhabit is inevitably one of fusion: after all, where else can you find clubbers wearing baggy pants and bhindis queuing up to buy ackee and saltfish bagels at 5 a.m.? The presence of black and Asian people in the UK has altered the anatomy of the country in countless ways, permeating every pore that ever sweated out a vindaloo on a Saturday night. Two or three generations down the line, the cultural melt is going both ways, and what black writers perceive around them is reflected fully in the literature, where a reference to *Gardeners' Question Time* might be just as relevant as a name check on pirate radio.

Whatever one thinks of the hype, few could deny that London, for instance, *is* hugely diverse, and people of different backgrounds, culture and class coexist and collide all the time. Although even today, as stories such as Ranbir Sahota's 'Chameleon' so wittily illustrate, what happens if they decide they want to marry each other may be another matter.

Against this backdrop I wanted to publish stories that were urban and edgy. By that I mean stories which crossed over into unfamiliar or perhaps unexpected landscapes – not in a way that conformed to any preconceived ideas about what 'black literature' should focus on as subject matter, or as writing that still identified itself as exclusively white either. Black writers have worked hard to have their voices considered solo rather than always as part of an urgent choir that requires them to sing in tune. I wanted to lay claim to any territory that demanded consideration, whether it was about eating and drinking – either too much or too little – the loves and lives of maverick musicians and magicians, or facing the future as we bury our beloved. And in the same way I did not think any author should feel precluded from writing about race, in that 'been there, done that, baby and bathwater' kind of way. If it is visible from the writer's telescope then so be it, the most important thing was that each writer felt free to set their own sights and depict what they see in the freshest, most evocative way imaginable.

The original impetus behind *Kin* was to showcase new talent, to provide a platform for writers as they are developing, and to help that talent blossom and bear fruit that could be savoured by all. The writers included here demonstrate remarkable range: from the softly insistent lyricism of Krishna Dutta and the elegant poetics of Francesca Beard to the electric energy of Gemma Weekes, riding the crest of the wave on her 'Gucci broomstick'. These are stories about our mothers, sisters, husbands, lovers, best friends and brides-to-be – even the odd vampire – whether here and now under Soho's beady neon or back in that hot, dusty summer of 1976. Each has its own unique eye-view and all are crisp and confident in the telling. *Kin* is populated by an array of fascinating characters – sometimes bizarre, always intriguing – whose stories I hope will captivate you as they did me.

Karen McCarthy

MARTINI
Heather Imani

I

It was the summer of '76. That fire-hot summer, when the grass in the parks was parched yellow and you looked along Kensal Rise and saw wavy lines of heat-haze and the roads were bumpy because the tarmac had melted and looked like it was boiling. The sun was blinding, frazzling our Afros, sending everyone a bit crazy. And perhaps because of the sun, Paulette got it into her head that we should go and look for Martini.

Paulette and me were in the same class at school. I was still thirteen, though, and Paulette was teasing me as usual about being the baby of the class because my birthday fell in the summer holidays. It meant I never got those little gifts that the kind girls in class always brought in for a birthday or at Christmas: foil-wrapped cubes of bath salts or Bronnley lemon verbena soap or pot-pourri. Soap-on-a-rope. Instead, Mum gave me either hankies or knickers, with new slippers or flip-flops or jelly sandals. And a lecture about being another year older and how I needed more than ever to study my books and *keep-weh from de bwoys-dem.*

I was moaning about that to Paulette. She said my mum was right.

'I don't check for boys, though,' I said.

'Hmm,' said Paulette. 'You think I never see you with TP yesterday?'

I blushed.

'You see you face – and I never even mention his actual name.'

'What?' I said. 'He only walked me to the bus stop. I never asked him to; I was just walking when he came up behind me – so in fact he never really walked me to the bus stop anyway; *I* was walking to the bus stop and *he* decided to walk there too. *I* can't force him not to walk where he wants to walk, can I?'

'Hmm. You so lie. You think I never see how you hook up your arms together and how your face was so grinny-grinny? I bet it was all *yes TP, no TP, three bags full TP* – '

I slapped Paulette playfully and she laughed at the fact that I blushed deeper and deeper every time she said TP.

And it was true: I couldn't hear his name without going all funny. I felt floppy and my head went kind of swimmy. The feeling confused me and to be honest, I felt silly. I thought it was something only the fool-fool white girls who read *Jackie* went through with boys they fancied, and that they only felt like that because they were stupid enough to believe a magazine saying they were supposed to.

'You better mind,' said Paulette. 'Two twos and you'll forget about your studies and it'll be TP this and TP that and you'll end up pregnant for him and drop out of school and you won't be any different from Martini –

people will think you're just a leggo-beas' instead of a bright girl who went stupid over a boy.'

My face burned. I slapped her again, harder. She was talking loudly and two Indian girls, who were sat on the playground bench next to ours fanning themselves with their hands, looked across, their faces like big-eyed dolls.

'Ow!' Paulette rubbed her arm. But she was triumphant. 'Truth hurts, innit, Hazel? Your mum's right: study your books and forget the bwoys-dem!'

The bell for the end of lunch break went and we peeled ourselves off the bench. Paulette pulled out her Afro comb and neatened her hair. Looking at her reflection in the dining hall window, she sighed. Her hair was flatter now than it had been in the morning. She sucked her teeth and declared the whole experience of this English summer disgusting because there were no trade winds to help keep everyone cool, like in Jamaica. I didn't see what that had to do with the sun shrivelling her hair, but since she went to Jamaica with her family every year, I thought she should know.

'It's so stuffy and it's like you're breathing in dry dust from everywhere,' she said.

That much was definitely true.

II

We had double science next lesson and after registration, we made our way up the main staircase of A Block to the lab. I was looking forward to the class because I liked Miss Halai. She was young and fun instead of old and boring like the other science teachers – all men. Also, we were doing a chemistry component and I enjoyed that more than biology (which girls were supposed to like best of all the sciences) and definitely more than physics, which I found dull and difficult, though I didn't like to admit that.

Our class congregated outside the locked lab, buzzing noisily and sweltering. A few of my classmates – not me or Paulette, though – were a bit whiffy from half a day in the same clothes. We waited for Miss Halai to arrive and let us in. A couple of minutes later, she bounced along the corridor, looking cool in an ice-green sari that swished under her sparkling lab coat. She carried her papers and a clutch of test tubes, and her single plait, which usually hung neatly down her back well past her waist, swung from side to side behind her. She smiled as she came up to us and passed the contents of her hands to Gary Burton, fished in her pocket for the key and unlocked the door. We streamed in and the wave of heat from the classroom scraped our faces.

'Rah, miss,' said Gary. 'It's too hot in here to work. Ennit too hot in here to work, Dalton?'

Dalton shrugged.

'Rah, Dalton, you let me down, man,' moaned Gary.

Miss Halai told us to open some windows. We obeyed, tussling with stiff old levers on the lower windows and pulleys to open the ones high up. We breathed exaggerated sighs of relief as cooler air flowed in from outside. Miss Halai started the lesson and the class took the shape it usually did with her: the ones who wanted to learn in a huddle at the front; those not interested at the back, doing their own thing, so long as they kept the noise down and didn't disturb the rest of us. The ones at the back were a few of the black boys in the class – Gary Burton and his crew – and the two white girls, Susan Wingate and Patsy Rowe, who mostly bunked off to go and smoke cigarettes. No black girls or any of the Indian kids went to the back. Our parents would have killed us if it came up in our reports. Sometimes, the boys at the back fooled around, touching up the white girls and we could hear them squeal and go *Stop it, stop it* - never sounding like they meant it. That was the only time Miss Halai would intervene. Mostly, though, they played cards. I never went to the back. Once or twice Paulette did – but never for the whole class. She wouldn't dare. She said it was because she was just curious to know what they got up to. But I knew she went off when she didn't understand the work Miss Halai set. Paulette was like me that way, not wanting to ask for help. But instead of giving up like her, I sneaked a look at what somebody else was doing to give me some pointers. That always worked for me.

Miss Halai was showing us some phosphorus, which was knobbly and purplish-black and stored in a test tube with water because she said it was combustible. She took a pair of tongs and picked out the phosphorus, when suddenly it slipped and fell to the floor. It whooshed into a small flame and we all went *Wow*! Miss Halai had to stamp on it to put the fire out and afterwards, there was a burn mark on the wooden floor where it fell. She checked the sole of her shoe for damage.

'Well, class, that just goes to show how dangerous – '

She didn't get to finish her sentence, because from the back of the class, Susan Wingate screamed and went, 'Christ! Gary!'

Miss Halai pushed a path through our huddle and we all turned to see what was going on. Susan's summer dress was up round her belly and Gary Burton had his hand stuffed inside her knickers. Before he realised that everyone was looking at him, he said, 'Rah, Dalton, I can feel all her pussy juices!' His voice sounding almost as if he wanted to cry.

III

The news spread like wildfire. Gary was suspended on the spot. Susan was sent home in a taxi with a note to her mum. They said that she might want to press charges for sexual assault. But the real talk was about how Gary had taken liberties because he'd been with Martini, who let boys do stuff like that, and whatever anyone said about Susan Wingate and Patsy Rowe, about them bunking and smoking and letting boys feel up their tits or whatever, they didn't carry on like Martini, so it was Martini who had corrupted Gary Burton, like she corrupted everybody, and if Gary got into trouble with the police or if Susan was traumatised for the rest of her life because of what Gary did, then it was really Martini's fault because she was the ultimate slag-bag, a leggo-beas' who got boys doing nastiness like this.

IV

First thing the next day was when Paulette collared me with a serious look on her face.

'Look, Hazel,' she began. She wiped the film of sweat on her nose; she said she'd run all the way up Okehampton Road from the bus stop to tell me this Very Important Development. 'A little bird told me – can't tell you who – that some boys went to see Martini after school yesterday when they heard what Gary did to Susan. Said they wanted to get themselves "piece". Nasty. Anyway, that same little bird – don't ask me who, 'cos I can't tell you – said that TP went with them.'

She paused for effect. My heart, lungs and stomach somersaulted.

'Bad, innit?' she continued. 'You see what's gonna

happen now? TP's gonna come back all corrupted and he ain't gonna wanna link up arms with you any more, that's for sure. He's gonna want you to spread for him and all kinda nastiness.' Paulette clapped her hand to her mouth. 'You poor thing,' she said and grabbed me in a fierce hug.

I shook her off. I was reeling from the thought that TP could have gone to see Martini. She must be lying. But why would she lie? Maybe it was just rumours. It was just the kind of thing that there would be rumours about. Of course!

'You're lying,' I blurted. 'TP wouldn't – '

'Hmm!' said Paulette. 'You see how it start already? You vex with me because I brought bad news. It ain't *my* fault! It's that Martini. You should be vex with her: she's the cause of it.'

She stopped and looked at me. I was trying to push water back into my eyes.

'It's all right,' Paulette said, softly. 'We'll go and look for her. Sort her out once and for all.'

The bell rang for morning registration and we spent the rest of the day not concentrating on our books but sending each other little notes, planning how and where we'd find Martini.

—*Operation Leggo-Beast. Target: Alison Brown, aka 'Martini' (we all know why). Should we round up a posse of Outraged Girls?*

—*No; this isn't general, it's personal. TP is involved now, so I'm involved.*

—*Well, I'm involved too because I'm your best friend and anyway, I thought of going to look for her first.*

—*Okay then.*

—*Where does she hang out?*

—*Well, she's supposed to love water, something to do with her being from Manchester. Didn't she say that in class once before she just went and dropped out?*

—*Yeah – What about Queen's Park then, by the paddling pool?*

—*Nah! Nobody's ever seen her in the park since she left.*

—*Does she still live near you?*

—*Think so.*

—*So, water – by you – Stonebridge Rec?*

—*Maybe, but there isn't any water there.*

—*Oh. Isn't there that canal that runs down by the flats, the other end of Stonebridge?*

—*Yeah, they call it the Feeder.*

—*Yes! The Feeder! Dutty water for a dutty leggo-beast. Must can find her there.*

After school, Paulette and me headed off down Okehampton Road towards Kensal Rise to get a 187 bus to Stonebridge. The sun was merciless. I felt uncomfortable in my flimsy summer dress and sandals, as if I wanted to strip everything off. Not speaking, we walked slowly, Paulette putting on lipgloss with her finger and tutting over the state of her Afro, picking at her hair as we picked our way along the roasting pavement. When we came to the sweet shop at the bottom of the road, we looked at each other and went in. We spent our bus fare on a fat Jublee each – mine cherry and Paulette's orange – and Paulette also bought a bottle of Fanta with her actual pocket money, which I never got. She asked for a couple of sheets of newspaper, which she wrapped her Fanta in and tucked in her bag for later. We tore at the waxy wrappings of the Jublees with our teeth, savouring the first suck on the huge, sweet chunk of ice.

It was going to be a long walk to Stonebridge.

'You should talk to her first,' said Paulette, breaking our silence.

We were coming towards Harlesden. My feet hurt. I wanted to go straight home really, but I didn't feel I could pull out of Operation Leggo-Beast now.

'Why me?' I asked.

'Well, you wrote on your note that it's personal for you, because of you-know-who.' She looked at me. 'Besides, you're half-coolie.'

'What?' I said.

'We should try to distract her, innit? And you should know what to say to her because you're half-coolie.'

Now I was just irritated. I found myself wondering why I listened to Paulette, let her talk me into things.

'What's that got to do with anything?' I asked.

Paulette shrugged. 'Martini's half-caste and you're half-Indian. You'll know what to say to her more than me.'

'It ain't even the same thing!' My voice was all screamy.

'I know,' said Paulette, calm as anything. 'But she's half-not-black and so are you. You've got more in common with her than me; I'm full black.'

I sucked my teeth and drained the last of my melted-out Jublee. I flung the wrapper into someone's front-garden bushes as I passed – something I would never usually do.

Paulette tucked her wrapper into her school bag and fished out her Fanta. She prised the top off with her teeth, wiped the bottle rim and offered me first drink. I shook my head and she took a long swallow.

'Mmm, still cold,' she said.

We walked the rest of the way in silence, slow, slow.

V

Martini was right where we'd predicted. We saw her from a distance, Paulette pointing her out with her empty Fanta bottle. She was by herself, prodding at something in the water. We could tell it was her because of her ginger-brown hair coiling out from her head like mad corkscrews. I felt a kind of creeping nervousness, almost sick. What was I supposed to say to her? We quickened our pace, and as we got within calling range, Paulette dropped back and pushed me forward by the shoulder.

'Go on,' she hissed, 'say something to her.'

I hesitated. 'Hiya, Alison!' I sounded stupidly cheery.

I looked at Paulette, who rolled her eyes. Martini turned her creamy-skinned face to look up at us.

'What do you lot want?' she said. She stood up. 'If it's about that Susan whatsername, it's got nowt to do with me.'

'Don't be daft,' I said, something taking me over suddenly. I knew without looking that Paulette would be rolling her eyes again because I said 'daft', like I came from Manchester too. I couldn't stop, so I continued. 'We were passing and we haven't seen you in ages – why don't you come to school any more? You're missing all the lessons and everything: you used to like Maths, didn't you – and you were really good at PE.'

'Don't come it,' said Martini.

'You're really facety, you know that?' said Paulette. She used her aggressive tone, her voice all bassy and out of the side of her mouth. She was taller than me and Martini and usually, people got a bit scared of her when she did that. But Martini didn't look scared at all. She smiled.

'So fookin' what if I am?' She turned back to the raw-smelling, slimy green water and poked in it with her stick.

'That water looks so nasty,' I said.

'Yeah,' said Martini.

'Doesn't it make you feel sick?'

'No. It makes me feel calm.' She turned to see the disgust on our faces. She smiled again. 'It don't matter what kind of water – even this.'

I was about to say that I had remembered she liked water, that that's how we'd managed to find her, when Paulette said, 'You don't mind nasty water because you're nasty.'

Martini laughed, turning back to the Feeder with her stick. 'Like I said, so fookin' what if I am?'

Paulette's eyes bulged and she looked at me for I don't know what – some kind of 'go' signal maybe, but I didn't have one. I wanted to know why Martini had dropped out and whether she was going to another school and why she liked water so much, even this disgusting water. And why it was she smiled and looked happy, even though she must know why we came to look for her.

A trampy-looking man with matted hair and a stinking overcoat shuffled up to us. He looked straight at Martini, a tall can of beer in his hand.

'You gwine free up de poom-poom for me tonight?'

Martini kept her back to the man. 'Fook off,' she said. 'Can't you see I'm talkin' to some people?'

The man stared hard at her for a moment. He looked at us too. He wiped his sweaty brow. I don't know what was going through his head, but he twisted his face into different shapes: angry, a beggy-beggy look, hurt pride, resignation and back to angry again. He took a swig from his tall can of beer, stepped up to Martini and took hold of her arm.

'Come, gyal,' he said. 'Me say me want piece.'

He sounded dismissive, as if she wasn't supposed to have said no, like she wasn't supposed to have any choice.

Martini turned slowly so she stood side-on to the man. She gave him a cut-eye look, slicing his ragged body slowly up and down from the corners of her eyes. A look of pure insolence, the kind of thing I'd get conked in my head for if I ever dared do that at home. She must give cut-eye all the time, I thought; it came so naturally to her. I was outraged and deeply impressed at the same time.

'Look,' she said, 'you must be thick or summat, 'cos I've told you about a hundred times that I ain't doin' it with you. If I wanna do it, *I* pick who I do it with. Gorrit? Now fook off. I'm talkin'.'

She slid her sidelong look to her arm where he was holding it, then tilted her head to look squarely at him. He released her arm and stepped back. He looked broken. Paulette sniggered. The man looked at all of us, witnesses to his humiliation. I saw his face change shape again. He raised his tall can.

'I bet I claat you inna you – '

He flew at Martini and she side-stepped him neatly. As he went by her, she brought her knee up to his crotch. The man bent double and dropped his can. Beer fizzed onto the canal path. Martini stepped out of one of her red shoes and hardly seemed to stoop before it was in her hand, the heel poised to strike.

'It's too fookin' *hot* for this,' she bawled at the man. 'But I'll smash a fookin' hole in your head if you don't get back in your cardboard box *now*.'

Martini was shaking but her eyes were on fire.

The man picked up his can and shambled off, muttering all the *claat* swear words, mostly about how *de*

*p___ claat gyal mek a r___ claat man waste off him good
b___ claat beer.*

'Whoy, whoy!' shouted Paulette, leaping up and down,
flipping her hand so her fingers snapped. 'That was
wicked!'

I couldn't help myself. I went up to Martini and
offered my hand, grinning. She shook her head but took
it, smiling. Then Paulette came up beside Martini and
smashed her on the back of her head with the Fanta
bottle. The glass shattered, a shower of rainbow sparkles
in the sun, and Martini gasped and wheeled towards me.
I yelped and half-caught her, then pulled my hands back
when I saw the blood exploding from the wound in her
head, the piece of glass sticking out. All I could think of
was how would I explain blood on my summer dress to
my mum? As Martini fell to the ground without my
support, Paulette kicked her in the face. She thudded
onto the path. I was frozen in the sun – couldn't move
my feet or my hands, although I tried.

'Get up!' commanded Paulette. 'Get up, you dutty
leggo-beas'!'

Martini scrambled to her feet, groaning, her cheek
badly scraped and her top lip bloody. She looked dazed
and pressed her hand to the back of her head absently.
She said nothing. Paulette swung her hefty right arm –
she did shot putt – and half-smacked, half-shoved
Martini into the filthy green slime of the Feeder. Paulette
went to the edge of the water to have a good look at her
there. I peered at her too, wishing I could make myself
look away. She wasn't moving and her eyes were shut.
She only had one shoe on and it stood out against the
colour of the water. So did the red cloud oozing from her
head. I was surprised at how shallow the Feeder was.
Paulette picked up Martini's stick and prodded her gently

with it. Martini groaned and stirred, the slime-water squelching as she moved. Her eyelids flickered, then she winced, sucking in a small breath. Paulette put the stick down on the bank, next to Martini's other shoe.

'Come on, Hazel,' she said. 'Walk me to the bus stop?'

VI

We passed the trampy man, who had seen everything, on our way back to the 187 bus stop. Paulette said she always kept some spare change for emergency bus fares home, and she reckoned this qualified. The trampy man stepped out of Paulette's way with an exaggerated gesture, going *Coo, coo, de gyal-deh bad-aaass*. We stood on the quiet road, silent for a moment. There was no one at the stop and no sign of a bus.

'D'you want another Jublee?' Paulette asked. There was a sweet shop just round the corner.

'I thought you only had emergency bus fare,' I said.

'Ah well,' she said, 'I've got lots of things up my sleeve.'

I asked for a grape-flavoured one this time. I didn't go into the shop with her to get them. When she came out, she handed me mine.

'We fixed her good, didn't we?' she said.

She paused for my reply but I said nothing. I squeezed the Jublee to soften it a bit and looked down the road. Still nothing.

'They'll think that tramp beat her up,' Paulette said.

We tore the corners of the wrapping off with our teeth. Paulette had bought herself the same flavour as mine. It was the first time I'd seen her with any flavour other than orange.

RAINY SEASON
Francesca Beard

'Select the right word,' it said. So she circles 'Ambivalent'.

Is that fair? Maurice would say she's confused. But what about other people? What would they think?

Insecure is not one of the words listed. The other words are: Lucid, Clear-cut, Confident, Positive.

Wait – she read the question wrong. The question was not about Anna at all. The question was 'Which is the odd one out?'

It's April. Today will be the sixth time in a row she's gone to a meeting. Maybe today, Anna will stand up, introduce herself, share, confess, be counted. She's crossing D'Arblay Street in a transparent mac. She's a ticking bomb, click, clip, clock, crack, crick, clack. She's wearing alligator heels. She's stampeding across the road, up and away, along the pavement, speeding towards the tube. Down the escalator she stomps, terrifying tourists and other lunch-time travellers. A businessman flinches as she overtakes.

'Hey baby, how you doin'.'

Anna nods to the Asian kid sheltering in the payphone. She doesn't mind harassment as long as it's respectful. African and West Indian men are generally cool but Jamaicans and Nigerians can be pushy. As can Moroccans and Eastern Europeans. Plus, Greeks, Italians and Pakistanis. Chinese men are all inscrutable. Anna doesn't recall any random come-ons from Orthodox Jews, but those Middle Eastern and Turkish men really wind her up with their lip-sucking and puss-puss calling. They don't want sex, they want violence. Done to them. Freaks, along with those English types, the 'Cheer up, Smile, Someone Die? Fancy a pie?' scaffolding brigade.

Anna explained this once to some guy at a party and he called her a racist. She would have argued the point, but his comment dragged a moderately good-looking face into irretrievable creepdom, so she just walked away.

Anna gets to the meeting late and sits at the back. Davide is sharing from the podium, his greying locks swaying as he thumps the lectern.

'I don't care how many times you've given up – I've given up more times than you. I've given up so many times it's in my blood. It's in my blood like drinking is in my blood and smoking is in my blood and smack is in my blood and coke is in my blood and whatever else shit you care to name – because once I've done something once, goddamn, I want to do it again!'

Twenty or so assorted recovering alcoholics and illegal substance abusers nod, murmur or clap their encouragement.

'But you know, you can choose your addiction – if you're an addictive personality, you can, I believe, at least choose your demon – and I choose giving up – I will always be giving up. I will forever be in the process of giving up – I am addicted to *Giving Up*!'

The small room erupts in applause. One middle-aged hippie whoops. Davide sits down and then his audience stands. Some move towards the back wall where there is a table with a coffee urn and a tin of biscuits. The others go into the corridor where they light up cigarettes and stare out the window. Anna mingles with them, she wants to avoid Davide, her mentor; he's seen her but she knows he's trying to give up smoking.

Outside, on the pavements of the Edgware Road, people start scattering for cover. The April rain falls for fifteen, twenty minutes and then, like a plumber, folds up this canvas of thunder and disappears.

Balanced on the equator, where water knows its mind and goes straight down, there is a small island. For certain months of the year, it rains here continually. The rain drenches the wild-haired Chinese ghosts that live by the frangipani trees. It hypnotises the Ceylonese merchants. They blink, blow fragrant steam off tea at the back of shops lit with naked bulbs. The rain falls from the palm umbrella held by a vine-backed boy over two English memsahibs. The boy's eyelashes are starred with water. The rain collects in the monkey-cups that grow tangled in the rough of the golf course. Underneath the monkey-cups, there is a small, pocked ball. The two English ladies, Valerie and Clare, are debating whether to continue on or walk back to tea or perhaps gin and bitters in the white-brick clubhouse whose window sills and door frames are painted thick racing green every first Wednesday of the month. One of the women is Anna's mother.

Anna is late. At Royal Oak, she feeds two fat pound coins into the machine and remembers she owes Maurice £35. As usual, there is no one in the ticket office. The booth which guards the exit from the damp platforms below is empty. When her train eventually curves through the rain into the station, the driver smiles shyly. Anna climbs on board, forgets all her annoyance and misery, leaving it for the next time.

In a cliff-top house overlooking the sea, Anna's mother kneels on the floor in a short white dress – a tennis dress with a culotte skirt. On her head, she wears a sun visor. As she moves, the plastic crown catches the light and throws lime-coloured blobs onto the pale wood floor.

'Always wear clean underwear,' says Valerie, as she rams a new pair of socks into the trunk with Anna's name on.

Anna grasps her mother's arm. 'Mum, I'm too young to go. I'll forget who I am.'

Her mother looks up dreamily. 'Anna, it's better to have loved and lost than never to have loved at all.'

What was she on about? Anna often thought about her mother's parting words.

'Think long, think wrong. The man I should have married was a debt collector. You could have been an East End gangster's daughter. Imagine that!' Valerie laughs her ice-in-a-glass laugh. 'But then, you would not have been you. I would never have had you. That is Not to Be Forgotten.'

'Valerie, will you write it down for me?'

Anna wants something pliable to remember her mother by. She imagines the soft paper, held over her mouth, keeping her warm in England, where it is always cold and people eat potatoes.

Valerie rifles through her bag and comes out with

what looks like a postcard. Into Anna's hands, she thrusts a heavy black-and-white photograph of a dark-skinned man in a straw hat standing in front of a fountain.

'The man I wanted was not suitable. They said I'd be throwing myself away. So Daddy brought me out here to find some army officer. I went with your father out of spite.'

Despite the jaunty angle of his hat, her father has a hunted look about him.

'Thanks, Mum.'

Valerie sighs and adjusts the sun visor. Little jelly suns dance on the white of her dress.

'Don't forget who you are or where you come from.'

Anna's peering into a compact, feathering waterproof mascara onto her lashes. Her eyes are locked into the narrow strip of mirror but she can feel the old man opposite, feeding on her face. She snaps shut the compact and glares at him. He looks away briefly, then, back come his eyes, like a wasp round a beer can. It's a free country, doesn't cost anything. Anna resumes her make-up, but defiantly. How dare he? A woman across the compartment looks, drops her head down. The train is pulling into Piccadilly Circus. As she walks off, Anna blows a sarcastic kiss at the man. He's still staring. His skin is ashen, the melanin starved on a sunless diet.

Maurice sits with his profile to the window of the crowded patisserie.

'I'm sorry I'm late,' says Anna, shaking rain drops off.

Maurice looks hurt and dry. Secretly, he has been waiting for only two and a half minutes. Maurice despises public transport. He cabs it everywhere.

'It doesn't matter. Why are you late?'

'I went to a meeting. They always overrun.'

'So why did you tell me five? You never learn.'

'Well if you know I'm always late, why did you turn up on time?'

'Oh God, I just had to get out of the flat. Jo hasn't called yet.'

Anna settles back in her chair for the long haul through Maurice's life, which is hair-raising enough to experience vicariously, fuck knows what it must be like to be Maurice.

When they first met, Anna presumed that Maurice was going through a moment of crisis. After a succession of these dramas, each one involving a lover or a therapist (once or twice, inevitably, when the two were combined), Anna deduced that Maurice was a crisis junkie, a manic romantic. The staggering peaks and troughs of his life were mood swings, induced by the lurch of his wagon as he hitched and unhitched it from serial amours. Maurice spends money on spiritual healing the way his lovers spend money on drugs. Now, having known him for seven years, Anna believes that Maurice is innocent of wanting to be disastrous. He is, or would be, a normal human being, but for some unlucky twist, whereby the beauty and intelligence that he was born with self-destruct into booby-prizes. Maurice talks about his life as though he were a critic, watching an over-written farce. Anna finds it difficult to share the same analytical fascination. She has, after all, her own problems.

She's replaying the thing with the old man on the tube. Through a panic cloud, she sees his clasped hands, frail ankles, charity suit. What if he was her cast-off father, come to London to look for Anna, exiled on the underground, searching the faces of strangers for his lost child.

'I've got to start my life,' she tells Maurice, choked. 'From tomorrow, no more drinking, no more coke. Jogging every day, before my NA meetings.'

Maurice isn't listening. He's texting. He's smiling at his own thumb.

Situated on one of the many oily streets that criss-cross Wardour, Dean, Greek, Brewer, in the so-called, self-styled heart of London, is Xen, a private members' club.

Maurice, holding the umbrella, says, 'I am a lump of nothing and not at all brilliant. This is Xen. This is where the gorgeous people go. I am here because they cannot be seen to just allow special people, they have to let in the lumpen prol of which I am representative.'

Anna fumbles with the wet keys. 'Oh, fuck off, Maurice.'

And Maurice, who is examining his face in the red-glass frontage, freezes in indignation. 'Yes, you're right. I *am* good enough for this shit-hole. Me, Maurice, I am worthy.'

Anna pushes open the door. 'No, Maurice, you provide contrast.'

They stalk into the dark club.

'So? You went to your meeting?' Maurice is restocking the fridge with champagne.

'Yes, Morris.' Anna is sorting mail for Helen, junk, bills. There's something for her, c/o Xen, from an old address. It's an airmail letter – she jags it open with the oyster knife – from Valerie.

Darling, I asked Stella for your address. Don't be angry. Poor Grandpa has died and left you some money. We are family after all. I'll be in London for Christmas – is the Ritz utterly overrun with Arabs?

'Don't call me Morris,' says Maurice. 'How was the sharing?'

'Oh, great,' mutters Anna.

Maurice frowns, waves his arms over his head.

'Um, hel-lo. Great? – and what did you say? – Hi, my name's Anna and I do less drugs than anyone I know? – Excuse me, why are you even going? You spend your entire life in a private drinking bar they call "the dealer's choice". And, Ms Anonymous, you don't even buy drugs. Which reminds me, you owe me money. I'm not bankrolling your little habit.'

Anna grips the letter, turns to fucking share, catches sight of herself in the mirrored bar. Jet hair sleeked into a high, tight, knot. Burnt-sugar lips. And Maurice, with his bronze throne-room head, his coiled body. Exotic animals decorating an exclusive watering-hole. They could be South American or North African or East Asian or West Indian. They could be Mongolian. They could be from anywhere.

On the island where Anna was born, the people are half-melted brush strokes of brown, yellow, red, grey. All the human colours. People take shape when the sun goes down, they move around. Children come to the stalls for currypuff or sugarcane. The rickshaw men sit by the storm drains, waiting for the opium vendors. The pawnshop owner shouts for his wife to take over and runs upstairs to join the 24-hour mah jong game. People swirl in and out of that room like silt in water. Only the ex-pats disappear to the isolated houses up on the hills, where they drink in wood-lined rooms. All the white people invisible, except for one. Under the frangipani trees, there is a new ghost, the colonel, rattling his empty glass towards the moon.

Anna leans on the bar, watching Maurice open the penultimate oyster. The water splashes from the tap into the sink. Drops fly out of the stainless steel and splash his white apron and pale buckskin shoes.

'Those are really stupid shoes to wear for that,' she says.

Maurice looks up in triumph as the oyster gives up the ghost.

He offers it to her and takes one himself.

She squeezes lemon onto the naked, grey muscle. The juice tingles her cuticle. She imagines the oyster cringing. With a forefinger, she prods the dimpled, satiny flesh, moves her lips to the gritty shell, tilts, sucks a mouthful of salt water and then, the oily proteinous plum slips down her throat.

'We need something to drink. Come on, I'll say it was me.'

Anna pulls an opened bottle of Pouilly Fuissé out of the fridge. The wine smells sharp. She takes a slug, rolls it round her tongue to warm it. The alcohol lifts the oil of the oyster from her taste buds. For three seconds, Anna's brain is in her mouth, thinking in salts, sugars, enzymes, complex fatty acids. For one moment, she is in the present.

'I hope Helen doesn't come in early.'

'Relax, have that one. The really fat bastard.' Maurice picks out the plumpest oyster, offers it to Anna.

'I don't want that one. It's too big. It might come to in my stomach. It's probably developed a brain. It might have a soul.'

The oyster disappears with a slurping sound into Maurice.

Anna selects a middling-sized, uninspired-looking mollusc.

'I'm not even sure I really like oysters,' she says, wincing as it goes down.

It's five minutes to midnight and Anna is sitting behind the bar. She pouts cinematically, cheekbones rising molten bronze, lips luminous with glamour. No one is looking. She slides off her stool and saunters over to one of the booths. Roland and Sandra own an advertising agency. They are drinking pepper vodka.

'Try some,' says Rolo and pushes his glass over.

'I've been drinking wine.'

'You can drink vodka after wine,' says Sandra.

'Pepper vodka is brilliant,' says Rolo. 'It's brilliant because it's like a liqueur, it gives you a little mini buzz every time you take a sip, it's nice to drink if you don't want to drink volume, just to get the buzz, but' – and he leans forwards, lifting his glass, forefinger extended for emphasis – 'the brilliant thing is that it's savoury. It's clean.'

Anna takes a sip from his glass.

The vodka is indeed deliciously savoury and clean-tasting.

It's a quarter to two. Joe Harness shakes his golf umbrella on the monogrammed entrance mat, wants to sign in three guests.

'Many people in tonight?'

He's dwarfish in a huge silver-camouflage puffa. Anna opens the visitors book as Joe peers round the door.

One of the guests – a granite cherub who could be Joe's brother – stabs a wet finger up at her and says, 'I know you. Where do I know you from?'

'It's Sade,' says Joe and winks.

'Fuck off, mate, I know her from somewhere.'

Anna smiles into the gap between Joe and Joe's lookalike guest. She tries to keep still, look as much like herself as possible.

'Are you a mate of Davide's?' asks the cherub.

'Davide who?' says Joe.

'Davide – model/actor Davide. Does a bit of supply on the side. You know. The older geezer, half-caste, looks a bit like Bob Marley.'

'Bob Marley's dead.'

'Yes, mate, I know that. He looks like Bob Marley if he was alive, but older. Grey-haired. Distinguished.'

'Oh, that one. We got him on our books. Not a lot of demand for that look. Shame, good geezer,' says Joe, ducker, diver, director of promos and heir to half of Lancashire.

As if she were Helen, standing on the other side of the room, Anna sees herself talking to the men. She must be careful not to be rude.

Anna wanders through her small flat, leaning into empty corners, switching on lights. She clutches the airmail letter over her mouth, sucking the paper, breathing in warmth.

Undressing, Anna sees her mother's body in the mirror, and falls in love. She's a miser, an old man, unwrapping a rare black pearl. With gloating hands, she handles her breasts, her belly, the sheen of her hips. She wants to keep it as she sees it – stilled, framed in silver. She must remember who she is. She has to change, she has to stop living this life.

Anna lies on her back in Regent's Park. Summer drips down her throat, honeycombs her skin, searching out the melanin. Freckles open like daisies, the hairs on her arms eddy in grace. She shades her eyes to watch the children scattering screams of laughter and gravel. They race round the rose garden, through the Persian mauve, pom-pom peach, court jester scarlet. English strains faint in the haze, pink and soft as old ladies' cheeks. Overhead, the sky is a Venusian blue. Into it, the colours unfold. Anna knows that this should be enough; the colours, furring her synapses with mineral deposits, salting up the shores of her heart. But the problem with highs is that you just want more.

'Want some Badoit?'

Maurice walks to the kitchen, passing her a laced joint. The cherry glows and she sinks deeper into the crunchy beanbag. Warm waves break over the muscle of her heart. Through the open window floats the glimmer of other people's evenings: TV quiz shows, cymbal pan lids, frying meat. A small dog barks. Water sluices through a man's laugh. A beam of peachy light rests on the back of Maurice's shirt, slices her fingertips.

The needle skates on static as the record spins round, round, round. Maurice plays with the glass beads round her neck. Violet specks fly off his fingers, swim up inside her.

'We should leave. It's really late.'

Maurice smiles in a way she never saw before – like everything's going to be all right. And a laugh heliums out of her, delicious, warm . . .

The shadows swarm, seethe; resettle. What was it? Something about islands. Her breath ghosts the air and she twists under the duvet, groping her twenty-four-year-old body, with its thin limbs, pampered skin, missing ovary, battered liver. Last night was the Hallowe'en party and Maurice's send-off at the club. Shivering with shock, Anna realises it's already the afternoon, she's missed taking Maurice to the airport. The answerphone blinks red. She crawls out of bed, hits play, pulls her sports bra out of the laundry basket.

'Hi, Vampira, this is your *wake up* call! I'm calling your mobile, byeeee.'

'Anna, it's your best and only friend, remember? I'm at my flat, the cab's here in ten minutes.'

'Yo, bitch, you must have left already. I don't have my mobile on me. I'll see you there – Terminal 4.'

'Hello, darling...' Anna freezes, pulling on her hooded top. It's Valerie's voice '...I'm leaving a message on your answer-phone machine. It's your mother. Aren't I clever to get this number? I'll be in London for Christmas. I know you're upset, but everything will be all right. You'll always be my little girl. Goodbye, sweetheart.'

Stumbling towards the lake, Anna keeps her head turned so she can watch the sun unfurl its lonely orange show, contained within a patch of sky.

There are no days in winter, she thinks. They end irrelevantly, incidental to the people, hunched over, hurrying indoors, towards artificial light and heat.

Anna has started to exercise. She's been jogging nearly every day for two weeks now and she's still waiting for that glow of pleasure and achievement. She hopes that she might develop a mild addiction to exercise; nothing life-changing, just a psychological need to get that adrenalin high. However, so far, each time she pulls on her trainers, it's with dread. At the nauseous finish, no endocrinal glow comes to her mind, just 'thank fuck that's over'.

'Merry Christmas!' calls the homeless man to a passing car. All along Shaftesbury Avenue, snow is falling. It catches in the lights of the theatres and the fluorescent 7–11. It slows down in the halo of the yellow street lamps. It makes the distant neon of Piccadilly Circus mysterious, the end of the world. Soundless parmesan slivers of snow drift onto the pavement.

Anna balances, swaying on the doorstep of Xen. She doesn't feel cold at all. She feels all right. She'd like Maurice to be here now but he's in Phuket. She doesn't really know Clyde and Malcolm. Malcolm's all right. He's good-looking. She could go home with him. He has a nice mouth and a full bottle of gold-wrapped Cristal. She's dragged them out to see the stars because she needs to make a resolution.

'But Anna, it's Christmas Eve. You're meant to wait till New Year.'

'No,' says Anna, waving her finger slowly in front of his face. Life is precious, not to be wasted. She'll bless it with this rare liquid.

'It's really good,' she tells them. 'Shhhh!' She tips the bottle and champagne foams onto the snow, leaving a fizz of concrete. Malcolm giggles but Anna is serious. 'Is a toast. To my father.'

'Is he dead?' asks Clyde.

'No!'

No, but he's not here, on this snow-smudged ground. She needs to find some sky, to see the same stars that see him. But she can't explain, so she walks away, off the pavement, feeling the convex curve of the road underfoot. Drunkenness helps you to notice things like that. Anna's pleased that her brain, though slowed by alcohol, is still in tip-top condition. When you travel at a slower speed, you notice details.

'I must remember to go slower,' she says.

In the middle of the road, a taxi smiles its little

yellow flare at her. Available, it's available. She imagines climbing in. Take me home, please. Too late. The cab slurs past, its tyres making dirty tracks in the thin covering of snow. She wants to make a resolution. She can hear Clyde calling her back. Where is that bottle?

A heartbeat away, in the same curved snowglobe of London, ice floats round a sober-green bottle of Dom Perignon, bobbing in a silver bucket in a hotel room overlooking St James's Park. There, on the bed, between the champagne and the phone, Valerie sits, wearing a dress of oyster-pink crêpe de Chine. The room is elegant with map-shaded lamps. Secreted wall lighting throws spangles onto the damask tablecloth from two heavy crystal flutes, waiting on the table by the window. Domed and gleaming platters sweat patiently between the cool plates. Valerie has made up her face: mascara, powder, rose lipstick and a baby's kiss of rouge. Plip, plop, pit, pat, fall the tears, plump as raindrops, in her lap. The curtains have been pulled back to reveal an unforgettable view of London, on this postcard-perfect Christmas Eve.

Anna stares up at the sky and feels the bottle slip from her hand, emptying out onto the curved road.

It's so clear, all slow and silent. Too many colours, too much city light. Anna can't see the stars but she knows they are there.

The night is precious now it's wasted.

WHEN ENGLISH GIRLS HOLD HANDS

Kalbinder Kaur

Milla and me sit in the shade watching dark bodies in swaddling walk far and fast. The square has a constant hum, like halfway between wind through tall grass and the light bulbs back at the hotel. Milla looks up from her postcard to smile at me every few words, but when her head is down I can see the guy in the white vest, the one frying samosas in a cauldron right there in the grit, meditating on her freckles, adding them up. They lead up her legs and down her arms, brought on by the sunshine. I didn't send postcards or take photographs, that would make me a tourist when I was obviously the tour guide, the expert, not to be seen in markets where mini Taj Mahals are found.

'How do you spell banyan?' she says, smoothing her legs, oblivious to the storm this could cause.

'Is this a banyan tree, then?'

'You should know.'

And I should do but I don't, so I change the subject, instead reprimanding her for wearing shorts.

Men walk hand in hand around the station; such uncomplicated affection. Milla and me do too, but we aren't copying, we did it at home all the time, we did with all our friends. We never got looked at or laughed at, Milla could not be considered anything other than organic much to my frustration. People never assumed we could be lovers, and I wanted it at least to be contemplated that Milla could be in love with me.

'I'm just so happy that we're here, can you believe this?' She is still intoxicated; she loves the furniture and jokes about having the whole room shipped out. I wasn't impressed but all this was shiny to her, exotic. Her eyes polished my sight. Without her jumping on our woven sitting-table I would have asked for a different room, possibly one with a foam-filled settee. Yes, I make a show of my civility, for them and me. 'Look how far away I am from you, brother. I am floating in the air between nations, while you are firmly indigenous. Do you even know what that means?'

Milla springs down the steps two at a time, giggling ahead of me. I am left behind, held up by crisp women saying they knew my mother. I assure them they did not, that my mother had probably never heard of this town and came from a place at least fifty miles further east. My speech is clumsy and in the end I speak English hoping they can still unravel my disinterest. Milla is waiting at the bottom and grinning up at me, thanking me. I don't know what for but I accept. We run to the river, me following, and I'm thinking that I still follow her here, but I don't mind the same. I am the parent now and she is the child having to demonstrate independence.

She wants to go to the cinema, a joke between us. I take us, nervous, as I have never gone by myself – without subtitles. She clenches my hand, and thanks me again. We are the highest, 'backest' row. Above the labourers, who clap at scenes with motorbikes, and whistle at yellow fluttering saris.

We take the bus back, on my insistence. Milla wants to walk, past starving street children and determined fruit sellers; but she is soft plastic in the sun, and bends under my direction.

'Is this the one?' she says at every other bus, until we come to the place where I know ours will be. She likes the way I know things, I don't tell her how I know, but just that I do. I let her sit down.

'No, I'll stand, don't worry.' And with one arm I push myself towards a railing on the bus window, and with my other I push Milla down between two village women on the back seat. I cannot see her any more, I am folded between cottoned bodies, trying to slot in the best way I know how.

As usual the driver encourages more people to board than there is space, and the parts of me hiding from the breeze stick to my neighbours. I turn my head around twice, the second time we just manage to catch each other's eye. Her eyes are all I can see and a freckled forehead behind the arms and hips of others. I pay the conductor for us as quietly as I can, so people cannot hear that I am not them. The jerks grow more bearable, and unlike England there is no need to apologise for every uncontrolled movement. I begin to enjoy the journey, as I always do once we begin and despite the sweat that rolls off my head like fat raindrops I feel good, because I have a view and fresh air to breathe, faring better than those around me.

I didn't know what a tweak was before, but now I do. It is about mechanics; a twist, not a stroke or an aim at arousal. He tweaked my right nipple. The offender is a red arm, and it comes back to cup the same breast. I turn around and a respectable man is watching me, and an older woman behind him. People have seen, and they are silently watching me, judging me. I am afraid they think I want this. I shift position, hoisting my arm as a shield. Milla asks if I want to swap, would I want to sit down. I can't let her go through this. So I just shake my head and smile, and use the opportunity to see the rest of the red arm. He is a pair of thick black eyebrows, and heavy eyelashes, that's all that I can see even though his whole face is there.

I don't look at Milla again. I have to pass her on the way out. I let her out in front of me, and the village women who were by her on the back seat. The arm grabs my arse, both cheeks. I jut my elbow back, and thrust a few times. I feel it going deep into his front, but I don't feel like I've hurt him enough. I jump off from the top step, and push Milla to the side. He is more than a red arm. He has a handsome face, and he's smiling at me. I don't look back till we're away from the main street, and into the first corner of our newly discovered short cut. He isn't behind us. I can't place what I feel, I am afraid it might be disappointment.

Milla has been quiet since the bus stop, now she says, 'I saw.' I ask why she didn't say, or signal. I don't say that I had been protecting her, that knowing she was watching all that time makes me feel sick, that my sacrifice was obviously a mistake. I try to reassert my identity as expert, and say that I hadn't slapped him or made a scene, as I didn't want her to feel uneasy. I didn't say I was so shocked that I couldn't slap him, so shocked I couldn't speak as I bumped against his body, his hands on my hips holding me in place.

She tells me I was wise to keep quiet. She tells me that this is common here. With the crowded buses, and all. It's the heat. She had read in the paper at home a few months back, she had forgotten which one, but it was scientifically proven this type of weather makes the locals obscene. She says there is nothing that we can do. She has heard of men murdering women for much less than a raised voice in countries like these. She tells me we'll get used to it, and squeezes my hand.

The silence steadily dissolves into Milla's observations of the shopkeepers opposite the hotel as we go back to the sitting-table in our room. Milla kneeling on it, arms propped on the open window, looks down at the winding alleys, deciphering their secrets. I lie face up under the fan on the hard double bed.

TRICK
Gemma Weekes

I want you to imagine what she looks like. She has a bright chill about her like spring mornings. She wears pointy red boots and distressed denim, black hair swinging about her cheekbones like wings, folded. She has arse for days and legs for decades. Mind like the edge of a razor blade. Bing-BOP-BOOM!

This is where it begins, at the end.

I suffer, smelling her on my clothes. I don't know what it is to be here. I'm standing, paralysed, on the bottom step, with empty hands and reluctant shoes. Which is the illusion? My walking away or retracing my steps? I draw my heart like a red dove from beneath my hat. It flies back to her. Magic.

A flick of the wrist, the shuffle, the disappearance. The appeal of the trick is the distance between what you assumed and what you know – for now. Everyone needs to be cut away from the husk of their assorted knowledges, sometimes. It can accumulate like mildew, or like fat in the arteries. Everyone is in search of their arch nemesis; the One who'll liberate them from their own power.

Indigo, boarding the train. Imagine. Her perfume is
Contradiction. *She is smiling and adjusting her tiny
handbag, folding her limbs into the seat, more than aware of
the round, pink businessmen trying not to stare. Failing.
Developing little two-inch stiffies in their pinstripes. Beyond
them, in the dark milky eye of the train window, is her
reflection. Warped. She looks into the blurred image; her
extravagant lips and sharp teeth orange with the sweet blood
of a mango held lightly between her fingers. Completely
unsuitable for public consumption, she is quite aware. But
she wanted it.*

I visualise her mouth and again, cannot move.

*Imagine. They would like her name, she thinks, those soft,
bald white men, perched like boiled eggs in a row. Indigo
Waters – sounds like it might belong to an 'exotic dancer' –
maybe to a high-class prostitute. They would say her name
was clever and pretty – 'Would that be your real name?'
they would ask her in thin, educated voices. She would only
smile. Names, after all, are a powerful thing.*

*It is, though – her real name. Claudia, her mother, had
been a dinner lady who perhaps should have been a
poet, but was cheated by time before she could discover the
joy of evening classes. Indigo was her gift to the world of
literature, and Indigo does her best.*

*She will be gathering her clothes together, now. Smoothing
her hair. Shuffling my cards?*

I feel a jolt of sympathy for number twelve. *Indigo is not
the type you forget. She wouldn't, couldn't fade. You could
never wrap her memory in a handkerchief, blow on your fist,
poof! Gone into the air. No.*

That's her trick, and she does it very well. Shuffle –

Aaaah, he so cuute. He curled up and soft like a baby,
deliciously post-coital, skin all gravy-coloured with a

body like a boy model! He twenty-something and loose
with hope and sex, snoring into his Ikea duvet. Michael!

Yaaawn. Open crusty eyes, blink into the dimness.
Scratch your balls, pull the covers up to your shoulders,
reach for me – Wake up. It's me, Indigo, wiping you from
between my legs with your face (towel)! I've soaked it in
cold water and Palmolive soap and – what do they call
it? Female ejaculate? I'm leaving you, Michael – smiling
into the dark like an assassin. I'm singing Millie Jackson
under my breath, slip sliding into red satin, lace and black
Lycra from neck to ankle. Ms Waters is painting her lips
crimson, darling, wiping the shine from her forehead
with baby-blue Andrex tissue and flushing you down the
toilet. Flicking you out of my eyes. Coating my 'do' in
hairspray.

Are you gonna take that, though, rudeboy? Are you?

'Indigo?' you murmur, half-asleep, naked – winding your
moist limbs around the absence. 'Indigo?' The air is
clogged with her scent, the clock beating the rhythm of
her cruelty into the heavy silence. Sorry, babes. I'm gone.

'Yeah?' I answer casually, from the bathroom.

Pick a card any card. Yeah. Remember it, show it to your
friend. Yeah, like that.
    Shuffle – Shuffle –
    Right! Sliiide it back into the pack. Yeah. Just like that.
    Shuffle – Shuffle –
    BING-BOP-BOOM! – um –
    Is that your card, miss?

You hesitate. I mean, there's no reason to gwaan stupid,
right? Maybe she's just having a pee, or a shower, brushing

her teeth. Maybe she's just doing girl-things, you know, like girls do. But I've picked all my clothes up off the floor, Michael! I've taken out my 'Isley Brothers Greatest Hits' and left the CD tray open. What ya gonna do now? It's cold in here. My voice sounds funny, doesn't it, like there's laughter under her breath. Believe it – there is.

I appear, smiling, in the doorway, buttoning up into black leather. You look like some kind of black Jesus, don't you? With those little dreads like a crown of thorns stabbing the moonlight. You've got those wet eyes too, and delicate cheeks – too young – even with the stubble climbing all over your face and all that pussy on your breath. You don't know what it is to suffer! God! You make me tired. What the fuck made you think you could handle this, huh?

Swish, I whip the black wool scarf around my neck. Click, click, click, my heels dance a cool tattoo into the wooden floors. There's almost no depression where I sit lightly on the bed – near your face – smelling of cigarettes and perfume. I trail one sharp nail down the side of your cheek.

'How you doing, baby?'

'I'm okay.' You ask. Staring.

'Good,' I say; white, toothy smile slicing the darkness. 'I'm leaving.'

Huh?

'C'mon, Indigo, it's one o'clock in the morning. Ain't it a bit late?'

I laugh like jacuzzi water. Pat you on the head. 'I'm fine. Besides, I mean, I'm leaving . . . you know, like, for ever. It's over. Kaput. Finito!'

You don't get it do you? 'Ya funny!' you say. 'Now stop fucking around, and get back in the bed, Indigo. Who said I was finished with you, yet, anyway?'

My smile is a dagger, lips glossy red. 'Look, sweetie, it's over. *Over.*' I consider for a moment, 'These six months have been fun, but I'm starting to get bored.'

I stand, pick my jewellery up, slide my hoop earrings in.

'Indigo?'

'I'm not joking. Don't call me.'

'You can't be fucking serious! How you gonna chat to me like that . . . ? Shit!'

Is it cold in here or is it just me?

'What's wrong with you? Why are you doing this?' You're a foal rising on new legs, tripping over your covers, stretching to your six foot three and your sleeping penis and your shiny skin.

I say nothing. You cling like grime to my skin.

'Why?' you ask, blocking the doorway.

Why? Y is just another letter I'm afraid.

'Look, fuck off, Michael.' I stab, eyes narrowed and dry. I push you back against the door frame, brush you off my lap like so many cookie crumbs. Crush you into the red carpet under these four-inch heels. 'You're dismissed!'

You let me go. Don't you know I already belong to him?

Lucky thirteen, baby.

I know he's watching me – the Magician. I can feel it – even though the admission is probably enough to buy me substantial psychological care on the NHS. I can feel it, my life gearing towards change, towards him. I put a little wiggle in my step 'cos I know like I know my own phone number that he's watching and that he's closing in – somehow.

He's the first that can see me. It's time. How much longer could I go superimposing the Magician over

Michael's face every time he pushed inside me? The time is now.

I have gone out, Anne Sexton wrote once, *a possessed witch/haunting the black air, braver at night;/dreaming evil*.

She would know my kind – so why doesn't Michael? Huh? Indigo Waters, love, not prone to random acts of compassion or charity. He'll have a tattoo now, written in his face and into his body language. He's had his heart torn out and eaten, ego pissed on, complacency busted. Trick! Some girl – somewhere – has finally gotten her revenge, and Michael won't be quite so pretty any more.

Oh, well. What a freezing-cold night and me – *me* – riding my Gucci broomstick into the belly of spring! Riding out again in my very precise MAC mask yelling *'Trick or treat!'* That's funny. How 'bout, I'm a trick and a treat? How 'bout, I trick for treats, I trick for treats in trysts tarnished with tasty but too tender types, then treat tenacious pricks like tricks for kicks? Am I good or what?

Poor Michael. Just another story I haven't told yet, another poem leaking from the jugular. I'll recite his pain to strangers (if he's lucky), outline him in black ink. Yep, some girl, somewhere, is finally getting her revenge. It's always the same with men. They grin and they laugh and bump when they walking and avoid phone calls; duck and dive and procrastinate and prevaricate then (hallelujah!) when they feel like giving, then you s'posed to be
grateful!

You s'posed to look all sweet like Nia Long or somebody and smile and open your legs and your life and your mouth and your doors wider like it's all you've been waiting on. You s'posed to fucking watch Oprah and buy self-help books and thank your fucking stars, well I'm sorry. But I'm really not that grateful.

'You're so beautiful,' he'd say. Lovely. Perfect. 'You're so fine! Pretty! Sexy! You're so beautiful!' Wrapped in my skin like a taco. All men need is a little genetic good fortune, delayed but expert pussy, strategic cruelty and they can't see ugly if it's sitting on their face. They can't see me. Sharp and broken on the inside, like broken glass on high brick walls screaming *Do Not Trespass*.

Ugly.

I tip my cap at you, Michael. I stick up my middle finger! It's cold out here and I'm projecting my question into the night-time but sister-girl has no answers for me. She can't tell me where he is – the trickster. London is not her home. Here, she blinks all different colours and screams sirens under her breath. She's a crack 'ho' curled up under herself; a manky black cat, fur missing, purring with a metallic hunger; eyes half-slitted, baring jacked-up metal, plastic and brick teeth, skin a cracked ribbon of black roads worn grey. She like a poem twisted up in her own metaphors. Jesus.

I shiver as the first frozen raindrops kiss my exposed face. Snow in April.

Is that your card, miss? Are those your panties . . . ?

Kinda thrilling to think that without the streetlights and the windows – all this eye-noise – the snow would be invisible. Imagine this cool softness thickening the dark. Icing the world silent. I'm mesmerised by each snowflake chasing its shadow over the wet concrete. Lord, if Sky would open wider, maybe the Magician would come shooting down to earth like an arrow of lightning, and me wetter than the Nile. Frying. Bbbzzzzzz!

Thirty-eight minutes and a smelly cab ride later and I'm

home. Sinking into my solitude, combing the silence and the white ceiling for stories. Nothing works to banish the Magician, neither can I capture him. Seems like I've written him over and over but it's just no good. I've been going about my daily business like clockwork, but inside is this stillness... and in that quiet, I know he's just gearing up to speak. To appear.

It was about five-and-a-half weeks ago. The place was teeming with people that night he played the first trick. The air was heavy with smoke and conversation. You need a description, don't you, reader? Shit, *whatever*. Well, it was a medium-sized venue, painted burgundy and green and some other colours. It was a long room with a few tables and chairs and an elevated stage towards the damned front and a couple of candles lit and a bar at the back, and you know, just a run-of-the-mill bar in South London. Anyway, the point is I wasn't expecting him to appear like that, bigger than any of my conceptions of what a man could be, blotting out the sun like an eclipse. He pulled my emotion like moon-tides, scrambled me into free-range eggs. I was fried by those black eyes. They steamed hot and liquid like strong coffee. He wore black from head to toe. And me? I stretched, trembled – a pink neck laid across the guillotine.

He spied me on the other side of the venue, nodded just once and drew each of my steps towards him till I could smell the warm clean taste of his breath, told me – 'Think of someone or something really important in your life.'

Shuffle –

'Mummy dis is borin', I wanna watch *Inspector Gadget*!' Indigo sitting between Mummy's legs while Mummy torture her with the blue comb and slim tug of quick fingers, weaving thick hair into cornrows with Indian hemp pomade smelled so good Indigo tasted it once but it was

bitter

just like cocoa butter and 'How come, Mummy?' Now she staring out the window 'cos Daddy ain't come home for days, she tapping you on the side of the head 'cos you squirm too much but it hurts and Mummy can't understand with her head of black curls. Mummy cooking spaghetti hoops in a saucepan. Mummy hunched over cigarette and *Woman's Own* and her weak tea same colour as her skin. Mummy running for 38 bus with little Indigo working little legs overtime. Mummy broad face, hair pulled back but wisps

escaping

all over her head – blue skirt stretched over wide hips, white shirt gaping over breasts nestled in market-bought white bra. Mummy, with the corns and bunions like dunes rolling under cheap corner-shop tights, standing on the cold tile which she told Indigo never do without slippers in case she catch cold. Nostrils that flare and narrow eyes that go Chinee when she laugh, she always smell like soap and Luster's Pink Moisturising Lotion and Lulu 'cos fragrance is maybe the one thing she won't cut corners on. Mummy, Mummy, Mummy – voice, the sting of her angry palm, Mummy laughing, Mummy play-dancing in front of *Top of the Pops*. Mummy crying quietly look just like a clown with black streaks down her face, Mummy chucking all Daddy's clothes into rubbish bags, Mummy don't look too pleased, Mummy don't wanna play any more she look cross –

His hands were sunk inside my brain – so, so close. The Magician sucked all sound out of the room through black hole suns for eyes. He breathed stillness. The curve of his limbs was a song I knew by heart as he delicately finger-fucked reality with his sleight of hand and his card tricks and stealing numbers out of people's heads then BING-BOP-

BOOM. He'd seen me. He'd seen the blood beneath my skin.

Mummy yelling! Shouting, screaming at

Daddy, 'Who is this woman?!' Mummy shouting in her slippers and housedress, 'Who you think you are – how dare you – don't bring my child around that whore –

tired of your shit – didn't come to England for this!' Mummy shouting over his explanations, slapping his face over and over, scratching his cheeks yelling

screaming

'You bastard!' Mummy yelling in Creole, '*Vieux salope*!'

'Stop it!' Daddy yelling, guarding his face he push Mummy away, but Indigo's little red and blue

rucksack strap

get in the way and she falling – falling –

Mummy head bouncing off the banister then the bottom step – *Mummy!* blood

pouring from her scalp, Mummy moaning 'cos it hurt Mummy

Mummy

Mummy!

Indigo little legs too short to catch her, Daddy

crying

screaming, 'Lord, I'm sorry – I'm sorry – wake up – God, I'm so sorry

CLAUDIA!'

Wake up Mummy

'*Claudia!*'

Dead.

Felt as though I was sinking through the floor. My eyelids were stinging and heart beating and the world gone silent in that flashback and flashforward and it was the Magician. His skin was dusky, honey-coloured and smooth, hair too short to guess at the texture – curly maybe, thick. North African? Biracial? Some West-Indian African/Asian mixture? Deep-set eyes, slanted eyebrows, wide mouth. *I've seen you, I've seen you!* I wanted to shout, but had I? He swallowed me whole, told me to look in his back pocket. Through the familiar pain of my grief I reached my arms around him (in my normal flirty-flirty way) and did as I was told, inhaling him through the black wool.

I was shaking. Tears leapt into my eyes and on the folded paper

Claudia

written in a perfect cursive hand

Claudia

He'd written, and it could've been my entire story. He saw me! I felt dark and soft like earth, scraped into crumbs. And the floor fell out from under my feet. I screamed and laughed, and giggled insanely, brushing strands of that blunt-cut bob behind my ears, gripping one of his arms for balance. The room exploded with exclamations and applause 'cos it was just a trick – after all.

He gripped me by the shoulders and stared into me until the room was silent again with anticipation, everyone sensing the strangeness.

'Indigo,' he whispered. My name! 'Think I'm big enough to catch you?'

I ran.

Two weeks since I left Michael sitting in the wet

spot. He's given up calling. And calling. I haven't even had the energy to be mean. I just want my prosecutor, the man who's seen me. Who's seen beneath. I've been losing my religion slowly. It's been leaking out of this chink in my facade and into tangled dreams and I've been losing my religion like REM but Tori Amos is the one who sang it in my language so – drunk – on loneliness – shit!

I can't take any more of this! I gotta tell somebody that it's him: him – long fingers conjuring the sun from behind the horizon. It's him, laughing my eyelids open in the morning. It's him, breath whispering against my skin when the windows open. Him starving my kitty-kat into crying the night away; scratchin' at the glass. Scratchin' at my alone-ness. Him the kettle and him the rug! Him the floor and all the hard walls. Him the stereo and the TV. Him even me! I curl up and lick the night like a Persian and dream of him – thickening the dark. The night is thick with him, coloured by him, filled with him. He's swirling all around, laughing against my skin. My eyes and ears and nose are clogged with him. I got my left wrist thrown up near my ear, one leg over the back of the couch. I'm stroking myself into shaking over and over, lost in the crimson behind my eyelids, shivering, bursting into loneliness. Open my eyes to the cracked ceiling, the cold blue flavour of this illness. And it's just me. Me, with my soggy knickers and bad poetry.

And then it begins. I don't know how he got my number.

Read Message?
lycos.co.uk
like u in
tht rd dress

> grl. Don't
> lk 4 me I'll
> find u.

I'll look around me frantically, standing in the line at Sainsbury's, or waiting for a train, or at the cashpoint, or watching Ricki Lake at home. I'll look disbelieving at my red dress, or my blue jacket or my denim handbag or whatever it is I'm wearing. I'll look out the window or search crowds for the shape of his stride. Nothing. He doesn't leave a number, he doesn't leave an e-mail address. He taunts me with his proximity. He sees me! He sees me!

> 'You have 1 new message, 1 saved message. First message sent today at 21 hours 31 – '

'Indigo, it's me. Be patient, I do wanna see you. Peace. Oh yeah, and I hope you're not gonna eat all those doughnuts by yourself!'

> 'End of message. To repeat this message press 4. To delete this message press 7 – '

4

4 4 4 ...

Indigo – long slanted eyes like green autumn puddles. Her laughter like a penny for wishes – that bright splash and then ever-decreasing ripples, a flash of copper. She has high cheekbones and a high forehead, a generous, pouty mouth, long fingers ... accentuating her five-foot ten-inch frame with at least four-inch heels at all times. She likes the distance that her height brings her, walks lithe and subtly muscular like a snake. She slithers slivers of a smile to her admirers, and deliberately her tongue darts out to moisten glossy purple lips and taste the air for predators. She needn't worry, though. In most habitats she is at the top of the food chain.

Indigo is gathering up her poetry. She's binding it all together, all the wrinkled leaves stained with images. She thinks that she can exorcise me with her poetry, her secular prayers. She's downed two cups of coffee, put on yet another new pair of boots and locked the door behind her. She's had a long overdue pedicure, manicure and haircut, bought a new outfit. She's scraped herself off the floor and committed some of those poems to memory. She's phoned her (modelling) agent and said sorry about all those clients she let down. Paid off her store cards, cleaned the oven and the toilet. Sorted her wardrobe. Done her laundry. She's bound all her words together like makeshift splints to strengthen her limbs, and she's marching out to exorcise me but I am not the devil. And neither is she. Neither is she.

I'm waiting.

THE NEXT STATION IS OXFORD CIRCUS. CHANGE HERE FOR BAKERLOO AND CENTRAL LINES.

She waits until the initial crush of passengers exit, serenely stepping off the train only seconds before the doors close. Behind her, the lustful stares squeeze pudgy fingers into her back. Yuck. She bares her teeth and lifts one perfectly plucked eyebrow at anyone standing in her way until they free up her route to the Way Out sign. Thank you.

Ms Waters slices a path of long strides through crowded corridors, up escalators and then finally – thankfully – she emerges into the street and the chilly air. The cold doesn't really bother her too much, though. It's early March and she wears her red boots with a denim mini pencil skirt and no tights. Her long, black leather coat is open onto a punky-looking black T-shirt with its white logo and arty creases, her neck is exposed to the sharp, cold breeze. She smiles lovingly at the women who attack her with whispers and envious stares, giving up their power.

A couple of side streets later, and she is at the doorway of a venue where poetry will be performed. Where I am waiting. The bouncer and the man at the box office try not to gawp at her as she informs them that she is a performer, and leaves them standing in a cloud of Opium.

I knew when she would come and yet, when she enters, it's as though I've been waiting –

Somewhere. He's here somewhere. Suddenly all the corners haunt me. He's here. The corners have eyes and the eyes have souls. I'm counting the heartbeats between every line of my poetry, legs wobbling in the red boots, wondering if I click my heels together –

forever. She's like a glass flower, with a stem of broken edges. I know that she knows when I enter and share the room with her. Her voice is husky, sweet and broken like chocolate cookie crumbs. Shuffling my cards, I follow the trail. I follow

saying in a girly voice, 'There's no place like home. There's no place like home. There's no place like – '

her scent all the way to the stage until our eyes are locked, and my intent glimmers over her lips like ocean diluted by Vimto. She goes –

home,' maybe I'll wake up and learn where that is finally.

I follow.

'Who are you?'

  'Call me Mo.'

  'I didn't ask what the fuck I could call you. I said, who are you?'

  'Mo stands for Mohammed. I'm a Liverpool fan. I like Cranberry Breezers. What else do you want to know?'

  'I wanna know *who the hell you are* ... how you ...'

  'What? How I what?'

  'How you know who I am.'

  'The same way you know who you are.'

  'But I don't ...'

  'Exactly.'

  'Why're you toying with me?'

  'Because all work and no play ...'

  'Oh, shut up.'

  'Okay.'

  'Where are you going?'

  'With you.'

This must be the beginning. Or a beginning.

  Darkness is rustling in the corner. Street lights are spilling fluorescence through the open window, soaking the white, white sheets. Illuminated: an elbow, a wrist, a beautiful brown face in profile. Sleeping deeply, spit collecting at the corner of her mouth, hair in her eye, fingers spread over a pillow now funky with sweat.

  Indigo. Indigo. Indigo.

  Shuffled cards have missed each other and fluttered down to the floor and onto the bed. I collect them quietly, and stare for a moment at my rebellious fingers. Then – gone.

  INDIGO! Wake up!

  Darkness is ticking away in the silence, rustling in the

corner. It's morning, but the sun hasn't risen. Wake up. Stretch, yawn, blink the sleep out of your eyes; scratch at your face where the duvet has written creases into your cheek – wake up.

What happened? Blink. Slide up onto your elbows – *fuck*. INDIGO! DID YOU LET HIM IN YOUR HOME?

'Mo?' *you enquire into the silence. Afraid.*

I'm in the bathroom, washing you off of my skin. Brushing my hair neatly, buttoning a shirt over nicely developed pectorals, pulling my boxers back on. Socks, Levis. Hypnotising myself in the mirror. Leave, leave, leave. There is no other way to keep her.

'Mo!'

'Yes?' *I say, standing in the doorway.*

You led me up your stairs last night, and through the door in an aggressive silence. Not looking at me. I watched you sit on the edge of the bed and unzip your boots, the line of your neck as innocent as birth. You'd stripped off with tired eyes and showed me your slick body as if it cost £1.99 from Poundstretcher. As if it wasn't a miracle in flesh. Your poetry was spread and crumpled on the floor under your bare feet.

I picked it up but didn't read.

I sit down now, near your belly. Reach for my watch on the bedside table and strap it back onto my wrist.

'I've seen you before,' *you say, and I can see only the sheen of your eyes clearly.*

'I should think so,' *I laugh.*

'I mean, before that show...'

I don't reply.

'I'm leaving, now, Indigo,' *I say at length, easing into my jacket. I check for my phone and walk towards the front door. I don't want to leave. People like us serve as our own punishment. I wonder if you'll ever understand that your beauty is real.*

After the door shuts behind me, you examine the soft mess I made of your defences. Cracked open, there are no razor blades, no chunks of ice. Just scabs, and weighty presences, and shadows, and those steps, and that blood you never washed from your conscience. You've defined and redefined yourself as murderer. Destroyer. 'You're mine,' I said last night into your ear, shivering, rocking inside you. Hard. 'You're mine!' I said, and was silent about your beauty (which is power in watercolour), kissed your belly button and your breasts, cuddled you like a child.

'You're soft as butter,' I said.

But who, really, is the broken one? My hands are empty. I'm standing on the bottom step and – suddenly – you're holding all the cards. I forgot my favourite pack on your rumpled sheets and leaving something behind has never been in the plan. I've left all my suits behind and I don't know what I'll wear. I've defined and redefined myself as trickster.

Indigo. Are you smoothing your hair, picking your clothes up from the floor?

I draw my heart like a red dove from beneath my hat. It flies back to her.

I want you to imagine what I look like.

NEXT OF KIN
Barbara A. Graham

'How could you let this happen, Brenda?'

'That don't help, what's done is done.'

'Oh, okay if that's how you feel, then what's the problem? What have the last two weeks been about?'

'I know, I know.'

'Well, we're almost there now, so we might as well see this through, and I don't mean make any decisions. We'll just ask the right questions.' Veronica produced a neatly folded square of yellow paper from her bag.

'I'm just being practical on your behalf,' she explained at the sight of Brenda's face as she read. 'You're going to have to think about this seriously 'specially in the long term and you need to do it quick. You've wasted two weeks already.'

The doors sucked in another volume of temporary passengers. Amongst them a female about Brenda's age with a Burberry backpack. She perched herself on the edge of a seat opposite them and continued eating a packet of crisps over the uncovered head of a newborn baby, nested close to her middle in a cosy harness. Brenda noticed her Tn-one trainers and gripped her toes in her 'Version IIIs' as if making sure they were still there, at the same time realising yet again that she hadn't thanked her sister enough, for anything. Right now she could hear her thoughts, she'd recited that lecture a hundred times recently, children having children blah blah blah.

'Don't say anything,' she whispered.

'I didn't,' Veronica whispered back.

The baby moaned its awakening as the tube slowed into their stop. The too-young mum rose to leave as movement from the chequered pouch accompanied fragile sounds. Absorbed by the crowd Brenda drifted along in the direction of the way out signs. Not conscious of their unforeseen crime someone stepped on her trainer. Brenda was vexed and stopped to check them both before she even began to wonder where Veronica was.

'Yo! Yo, B!'

Brenda looked across the platform and had no trouble spotting Clinton Davies. *The* Clint Davies that she and every other teen-year-old female at Newgate Comp desired, and he knew it. He signalled with arms and eyebrows for her to come over. S'funny, she thought, how he was always Clint Davies like there were two Clints on the manor and you had to use his last name to differentiate. He waited at the foot of the stairs wearing the blue to her grey trainers and a denim suit that told everyone a million times it was Moschino. Nah, there's only one Clint Davies, she thought.

'Hey, babes. Lookin' good. Lookin' good.'

'Hey, Clint.'

'Wha's 'apnin'? How you jus' scarce all of a sudden?'

'Ah, you know, I bin hangin'.'

'I asked you fren dere for you, more than once.'

'Who? Amma?'

'Yeah, das right. So where you headin'?'

'I was just ... going to see what they had in the sale,' she said, thinking fast and acknowledging his Probito bag.

'Yep, a man's gotta have his garms. They ain't sayin' much doh.'

'Sale innit.'

A tube pulled in and waiting and existing passengers exchanged places in an unrehearsed dance. Brenda's phone rang. She viewed the screen then killed the call.

'So what you sayin' nex' one's mine, why don't we head back an' cotch at my yard, play two tunes?'

Brenda's phone rang again. She switched off, knowing Veronica's call would go to answerphone.

The tunnel sounded the approach of their carriage.

'How is your mum anyway?' she asked, stepping towards the platform edge in consent.

'You know always sup'n sup'n. She asked for you, you know.'

'Yeah, right.'

'Nah, no lie. It's not anyone that gets taken home to meet mums, you know.'

Brenda's heart bungeed off its platform.

'I still can't believe how you just disappeared on me. I thought me an' you was sayin' sup'n. I even bin down the sixth form block but dem girls said you wasn't about.'

'Nah, man, school's long.'

''Specially since I left innit.' He smiled his female indifference antidote of a smile unnecessarily.

'What you been up to since you left then?'

'You know, a man's gotta do.' His mobile beeped a message. He kissed his teeth as he read, not hiding from Brenda the fact that he wasn't pleased with its contents. Brenda wondered what she was doing there. Veronica was going to be maaad. Anyway, how could she even begin to deal with things? She'd messed up big time.

Above the colourful veins of the underground map the words of a poem pulled travellers back from the future their destinations compelled, into the here and now. Brenda thought of all the lessons she'd missed recently.

> *Love is too young to know what conscience is;*

Another message commanded Clint Davies' attention.

> *Yet who knows not conscience is born of love?*

Things wouldn't be so bad if she and Clint were proper lovers.

> *Then, gentle cheater, urge not my amiss,*
> *Lest guilty of my faults thy sweet self prove.*

. . . or even an item.

> *For, thou betraying me, I do betray*
> *My nobler part to my gross body's treason:*
> *My soul doth tell my body that he may*
> *Triumph in love; flesh stays no farther reason,*

Clint Davies kissed his teeth dismissing his messenger.

> *But rising at thy name, doth point out thee*

'Wassup?'

> *As his triumphant prize. Proud of this pride*

'No worries, nut'n I cyan handle.'

> *He is contented thy poor drudge to be,*
> *To stand in thy affairs, fall by thy side.*
> *No want of conscience hold it that I call*
> *Her 'love' for whose dear love I rise and fall.*

As the Central Line tube pulled in to Mile End station, an empty District Line train waited opposite offering them seats. The doors opened with a growl as if challenging the opposition for its prey. Clint and Brenda stepped out together in the direction of the open doors. Suddenly Clint grabbed her hand and basketwove a route in and out of the strands of fellow travellers, then leapt between the nearest open doors just as they began to close.

'Man, what was all that about?'

'Nut'n. I've just got a thing about sitting in the front carriage.'

This time his half smile didn't work. Brenda was annoyed that she had to stand and wondered again *what* she was doing. They emerged in silence from the tarred colon of the underground and daylight said hello.

Clint's mobile blew up 'Mission Impossible'.

'Aw, man,' Clint Davies despaired.

'Yeah.'

Brenda could hear the staccato tones of a female with a lot to say. She moved closer to the doors and leaned out as they opened, letting the air stroke her face. Her brow creased as she noticed the young mum with the kangaroo pouch jumping carriages. Clint Davies ended his call.

'What?'

'Nothing, I just thought I saw someone.'

Their silence becoming awkward, Brenda claimed the

seat the previous occupant had kept warm for her. She studied Clint, trying to see past his good looks and imagine him the playa she'd heard he was, but still she felt lucky. Feeling her eyes he looked over and winked, stirring everything dormant in her groin.

Familiarity stared at her from outside the windows, although appearing greyer than usual somehow. Brenda wasn't sure if her mood frosted the windows with its momentary melancholy or if it had more to do with the compulsory dust of the underground imprisoning the eyes of its hostages; forcing them to peruse ads and maps and each other and journey deep into the anatomy of their minds. At Upton Park Brenda sat up a little, alert to the fact that Veronica could be walking along the platform heading home. Ironically, it was the girl with the baby who'd already featured twice in her day that hopped through the doors, her hand protectively on her mound. She stood in front of Clint in a back-arched stance Brenda was sure she'd grown accustomed to not too many months ago.

'So what, you don't wanna know me now?'

Brenda shrunk in her seat, her heart racing four to a beat in perfect time with the tube's rhythm.

'Listen, Keisha, jus' cool, I neva jus' tell you I'd get to you later?'

As the tube gathered speed, so her heart raised its tempo helping realisation bruise her insides.

'Yeah, later like never, you bastard. Ah bin waitin' down West like a fool an I *know* I saw you at Mile End.' Hands akimbo, Keisha's neck danced an Asian dance. 'In fact if the guy in Probito never told me you'd already been in, I'd be waiting there now. An' I got the baby. I just don't believe you. You make me fucking sick.'

Embarrassed, Clint Davies turned to face the doors

away from them both. Then almost immediately he turned back again.

'Listen, Keisha, fuck you. I waited but you never reach, an' a man's gotta do.'

'Fuck a man's gotta do, you ain't nut'n but a bwoy jus' like my mum said, you can't do nothing for me or Kai. You couldn't even turn up to give him your name.'

'Yeah, das right, das *your* chile. I dun tell you do what you gotta do.'

'Yeah, an all *you* had to do was bring your fucking friends to the hospital to fucking show off like he's any qualification, now he's my child. Yeah, he's my chile an you ain't nothin' but a niggah.'

Brenda remembered Clint leaving her one day in the summer holidays to visit his mum in hospital. She had offered to go with him but he'd said she wasn't up to too many visitors.

'Das right, Keisha, I'm a niggah, full blown and fucking proud of it. Get it. Your baby daddy's a niggah.' He was all up in Keisha's face and not looking too attractive from where Brenda was sitting.

'Nah, it ain't nothing like dat, Clint, this is *your* son. We're here for life. Baby, Mother whatever. My chile needs a daddy. I never had him to go without anything.'

'Listen, Keish, it weren't even no long ting but these tings happen. Jus' cool, man. You're making things harder than they need to be. '

No long ting, Brenda thought. That sounds familiar. His suggestion, after the first impetuous occasion. Her agreement. Casual. No big ting. Just sex. Her only condition that it was protected. It hadn't worked. In fact no condom could protect her from the hurt she felt now. They don't tell you about that.

'No long ting. I'm making things hard. I don't believe

you Clint Davies.' As if realising for the first time that they were there, Keisha turned to her audience in astonishment at what she'd just heard. She looked straight at Brenda who had a front seat, shaking her head.

'My brothers warned me, you know. Neil told me, I was jus' too blind.' Her tears spilled onto her baby. She looked every part the victim, no role play, childlike, vulnerable and wearing a wound no plaster could hide. Brenda felt sorry for her and her baby but even sorrier for herself. Keisha's baby moaned his awakening. The opening doors drowned the sound of their continued argument as Brenda slipped off at the last minute. She didn't want to hear any more. She walked towards the exit as the tube started out of the station. Clint's eyes held hers as he noticed her. Keisha occupied Brenda's seat, her head bowed.

Brenda had time to think on her way home and took the long route, which allowed her even more. She avoided the High Road where she knew her friends would be furnishing the local pizza parlour, busy debating other people's business and doing nothing at the same time. As she approached home she realised how events on the District Line had long extinguished from her mind the fact that she'd deserted Veronica in Oxford Circus after she'd taken the day off work. Feeling bad about this, she called to soften the blow. Spewing everything out at once, she didn't give Veronica a chance to start.

'Hello, Vern, it's me. I'm sorry, I needed time to think. I'm done, I've made up my mind . . . and we'll speak when I get home, I'm not far now. Bye.'

As she put her key in the door she decided to close her thoughts on the day's events. Her mind was made up.

Veronica appeared from the back room in her work clothes and slippers; her reduced height revealing a fullness her regulation high heels disguised.

'Well?'

'Okay, you win.'

'It's not about me winning, Brend, you *need* to be sure about this. I know I haven't hidden how I feel. But I need to know it's your decision. I'm here for you either way.'

'I know.'

Two steps later Veronica hugged her sister for herself and their mum and dad. For once Brenda didn't complain about her messing her hair. Veronica looked up into Brenda's eyes. 'You won't regret this you know, Sis.'

Brenda didn't say anything. She wasn't really in the mood to talk, so punctuated Veronica's repeats of what she'd said time and time again with the right responses in the right places, while making a cup of hot chocolate. She wished – not for the first time – that her mum was there to do it for her. A hot bath didn't prevent the night-time eclipse on her daytime decisions. The darkness cast doubt in a halo of confusion about her head. She thought about Clint Davies and his 'people minding our business, keep it on the down low, no complications' body talk. Had she made the right decision? Changes weren't always the end of the world. Thoughts bounced around her brain like bluebottles buzzing around a burning light bulb. Veronica was right, she was better off leaving the whole episode behind. She thought about her mum and dad. Would they really have been proud if they knew it all? She thought not. She didn't want to end up needing him like Keisha . . . but then that could never happen; as far as Clinton Davies was concerned she'd left her feelings for him somewhere deep in the glands of the underground. Despite all her efforts Keisha and her son would not leave her alone. Veronica was right – she'd wasted too much time already. Clint Davies. Mum and Dad. What if anything should happen to Veronica? That's when her life would be over. She'd made the right decision. Hadn't she?

Veronica woke her with a cup of tea and invited the daylight in, parting the Forever Friends curtains bought by their mum, which Brenda had long grown out of. Brenda squinted and buried her head in the comfort of her covers.

'How d'you feel?'

'Tired.'

'Did you sleep?'

'Some.'

'I managed to get through. They'll see us this morning at eleven.'

'You didn't even ask me. I feel sick.'

'It's nerves. Drink the tea.'

'What time is it?'

'Nine, so you better get up. I'm gonna call work.'

'I've changed my mind.'

'Drink the tea.'

Everything went well just like Veronica said it would. Veronica insisted on explaining about Mum and Dad and already she had an appointment booked with the counsellor. She'd picked up quite a few leaflets and the whole thing seemed positive and focused on the future, which helped to convince her it was the right thing to do. By the time she was on her way home and had begun to digest everything, she could almost admit to herself that she was looking forward to it. She might even get a backpack like Keisha's; she would no doubt need it. After a quick coffee together Veronica had gone to work and managed to take all the paperwork with her. The tube soon came and Brenda lounged in seats that reminded her of leftover orange and brown liquorice allsorts, relaxing in a front-room position that Veronica would have reprimanded her for, saying she's not a boy despite all Daddy's prayers and she'd have gone into the whole skirt and frock thing but Brenda didn't adjust herself, she decided it was relief leaving her body. She considered going down the sixth-form block to check them girls but the thought of running into any teachers and having to explain her absence let alone the fact that she was leaving made it easy not to.

Naturally, the journey home reminded her of her last, so she decided to change route. On her way to the next platform she remembered that Amma had her Walkman and made a mental note to get it back. She hadn't heard from her in days, but then she hadn't wanted to, her problems had seemed too serious. Brenda watched the tube arrive from the mouth of a screaming tunnel and felt the eyes of the driver appreciating her as he slowed to stop, serenading her with his music of metal and grease. Slimy, she almost said out loud. The fact that he wore dark glasses and a reversed cap just like all the other pensionable kerb crawlers forced her to smile and she imagined how each station must seem to him like a sunny day in a different city and he was driving a limo longer than anyone else's.

The front carriage was empty enough for her to resume her relaxation for what in all honesty seemed like the first time in weeks. She liked to tell herself that she didn't do stress because she wasn't going to let it do her, like it had done her dad after a twelve-hour shift. No way was she going out like that but something had definitely left her that morning.

Reassurance came in a line from an ad selling life insurance, of all things.

Love is pointless. Love does not make you money.

There is a God, thought Brenda. For me to have got into this carriage and seen those words today. There is a God and he's texting me. I *am* doing the right thing.

Brenda tried a few times to call Amma but couldn't get through so she jumped slightly when her phone vibrated in her breast pocket. She read the screen, Buffting.

'Shit, it's him,' she said out loud.

She locked off and tried Amma again so Clint couldn't get through.

'Hey, girl, whaagwan?'

'Just chillin'. I'm down the block. Where you bin? Are you ever comin' in again?' Amma joked.

'Nah, 'fraid not.'

'Yeah, right. Your tutor gave me a message to give you but you been scarce man an' your phone's been locked. How much was the bill this time?'

'It ain't about that. I got sup'n to tell you.'

'Yeah, an I got sup'n to tell you. You never guess who I saw.'

'Who?'

'Down Stratford Centre.'

'Who, Amma?'

'Big, big holin' hands yuh know.' Amma laughed her signature tune.

'Come on, Amms, spill.'

'It's your fren dere . . . what's 'er name?'

'Amma, you're killing me?'

'That girl in your English class, the one who tink she's soooo nice.'

'Rochette?'

'Yeah, an' guess who she was with?'

'Who? Come on, Amma, don't do this to me.'

'Simon.'

'Who, Dukes?'

'Nah...Johnson. Aaaaaagh!' Amma burst into her louder than life laugh and Brenda could see her splayed all over the sixth-form sofa, exhausted from it.

'What, Pokemon? Nah your lyin', Amma. Big big holin' hands for true? I don't know whether to believe you or not.'

'Brends, it's true big time. Ask CJ if you don't believe me. He was there. So yuh comin' down or what?'

'No, you come round.'

'Nah, I'll meet you in pizza.'

'Amma, I'll see you round mine later.'

'All right. I thought you said you had sup'n to tell me anyway.'

'Yeah, an' bring the Walkman. Laters.' Brenda ended the call hoping her friend had got over her own life-threatening crush on Clint Davies.

Veronica dressed Brenda's bed, which had been airing for the last two months. In her absence she had decorated her room a safe, creamy beige and moved the furniture around, even bought new wooden blinds. It was time. Time for a new chapter in their lives. Mum and Dad were gone and keeping things the same wouldn't bring them back. She shook life into the new duvet as she pondered the last three years. Dad's accident had been a shock and Mum's stroke six months later had brought their lives to a standstill, but it had happened. Yes, it had been tough since and Brenda had shown signs of... signs of what she thought... rebelling? Wasn't that to be expected? Any reaction would have been understandable, however extreme. No, Brenda was a good girl. Hopefully now they'd passed the worst. There was a time when she thought she'd never get to the point of wanting to move on but preparing for Brenda's return today seemed to finally allow her to edge unhappy memories into the past. She'd made the first tentative withdrawal from Dad's settlement money. £253,000, it had come through just in time. They'd lodged the cheque with her solicitor in settlement out of court the day before the hearing. She wondered how many fit-for-use forklifts it could buy J B Corks plc.

The accident had severed four lives, two without burial. Brenda had reacted by throwing herself into revision for her GCSEs. As a result, she got the excellent grades expected of her but didn't seem to be interested in anything once the exams ended, no matter how hard Veronica tried. In desperation she had contacted Amma to suggest that she and Brenda go and pick up their results together, having a quiet word with her at the same time to see if she couldn't get Brenda out of herself. The two of them had come home in such high spirits; Veronica pictured them skipping all the way hand in hand like they used to. She'd guessed their results must be good but Amma's read like a list of unhealthy additives and she refused to go home, claiming to be scared. They'd spent the afternoon all girls together, laughing at CJ's hair in old school photos, reminiscent of the days when Veronica used to pick them up and nothing was more important than being a milk monitor. It was the first time the house had known laughter in what felt like years and even now Veronica smiled at the thought. Amma's personality was always an asset in a bad situation, even her own. Although when they started sixth form, Veronica found she'd begun to regret encouraging the friendship and spent a lot of time cussin' Amma and her under-achievin' pizza-house posse. She wondered whether the 'fun' (as Brenda had put it) hangin' out with the local Shabbas (as her mum would have put it) instead of going to lessons, was Brenda's way of making sure she took time out to live after experiencing the interruption of death. Her delayed way of grieving maybe? She realised they'd never actually taken time to grieve together and plumping the pillows she'd just tucked safely into the transformed Forever Friends pillow slips, she wondered how she could address this two years too late. Maybe when Brenda came home they could go to the cemetery together. But then, she sounded so positive in her phone calls nowadays maybe there was no need to worry.

How she'd survived the stress of the months before Brenda left, Veronica didn't know. She breathed a continued sigh of relief recalling how she'd been stupid enough to think the worst but, thank God, no, she wasn't pregnant. The answers had come on the day of her tearful confession which began with the bombshell that she hadn't been going to sixth form because she was bored with it and how her life was going nowhere. And yes...if she remembered correctly that was the same morning the letter finalising the court date had crash-landed on the doormat. The shock of finding out that Brenda *had* in fact got three A Level passes, did not have to resit and could have gone to university, soon became pleasant relief. Then after weeks of coaxing there was the day when she disappeared on the way to the first interview, leaving her stranded in Oxford Circus to purchase yet another pair of shoes on plastic. Veronica struggled to stuff the duvet into a new damask cover. For the hundredth time she pondered over why Brenda had lied to her about her results; maybe she'd made it difficult for Brenda to talk by going on so much about her hanging out in the pizza parlour with Amma and her intermediate-level friends. She probably knew she'd try to convince her to go to university, after all that's exactly what she did do for the two weeks it took after finding out. The seventeen years between them meant that Veronica had always assumed more than would have been expected of her in terms of delegated parental duties but she'd not had to bear the sole responsibility she felt now. She placed two new pillows on top of the old ones and was pleased with the room's new look. Perhaps she'd do her room next and work her way around the house, after all she could afford it. It would give her something to do now she had no one to cook for and the evenings seemed so empty. She'd discuss it with Brenda. Didn't want her to feel she didn't belong any more. It pricked her conscience that she had not told Brenda about the first offer in settlement of their father's death, but knew that any number of thousand pounds would sound like a great deal of money to an eighteen-year-old. These thoughts consumed her until memories of the day they spent shopping for new clothes and a Burberry backpack brought her up to date.

She placed a framed photo of Mum with the two of them on the newly painted shelves. Studying it, she recalled the day they'd gone to cousin George's wedding. Mmm ... happy memories she thought, wishing Mum was here to enjoy the money with them: she deserved her fair share. Veronica sighed, deciding the money would secure a future for Brenda and her children even if it was too late for her. Okay, she'd survived but she wasn't the successful role model of a teacher Mum always wanted her to be. Finally, she put the small photograph of their father back by Brenda's bed where it had always been. She gazed at it, hating the effect even a small photo of him had on her, until the telephone rang, jerking her back into the present.

'Hello.'

'Hello, Verni, how yuh do?'

'Hi, Aunt B, I'm fine. How are you?'

'Yuh know de same ole pain dem a lick me hevry day. Ah soon gaan.'

'You're not going anywhere and I don't need to hear that right now. How's Uncle?'

''Im ah right. Where's Brenda, how she is?'

'She's not here, Auntie, she's away studying.'

'She not going to school any more?'

'No, she left school. It's a long story.'

'She behavin' arself?'

'Yes, she's okay. She changed her course. They didn't do the one she wanted to do at school.'

'Dem neva kick ar out?'

'No, Auntie. She's doing well, she's going to uni-ver-sity.'

'Suh why she ave to gaan so far?'

'It's not that far, I just wanted to get her away from the friends so she could concentrate, you know what youngsters are like.'

'Verni, yuh shure she nuh prignant?'

'No, she's not pregnant, Auntie.'

'Only when you did goh weh fi study lickle while you come back wid baby. Yuh nuh tell ar yet is it? Verni, mark my words, don't say ah gaan too far ina yuh business, is not everything good fi eat good fi talk; don' tell ar till she dun study, cah yuh wi mess up de pickini'ed. Ah know 'e was yuh farda, Verni, but 'im was a wicked man, das why 'im dead suh bad.'

Veronica had always hated the fact that Mum had told her sister, but over the years she'd come to understand. She still lived a lie that she would never share with anyone else but there was no way on God's earth she was going to let Brenda find out that she was too.

'Don't worry, Auntie. Listen, I don't want to stay too long in case she's trying to get through.'

'Oh, you should get call waiting dear, I 'ave it. Yuh neva see de hadvert pan de telly. BT got it on free trial, then yuh give it up, you know how it goh.'

'Okay, I'll try it. Say hello to Uncle.'

'Ah right ah gaan. Tell Brenda hello.'

'I'll get her to call you, Auntie.'

'Ah right, bye.'

'Bye.'

Veronica could see her daughter's silhouette approach the front door through obscure glass. She swallowed hard sending neglected emotions into retreat. She opened the door and as they hugged without speaking Veronica burst into tears. After convincing Brenda they were 'I've missed you' tears they chatted easily, like the sisters Veronica now felt the guilt of pretending they were. Brenda's eyes were alive with campus life and the lack of time she now had to sculpt her hair with gel, resulted in a new look, which lifted the curtains off her face. She wore it back in one, still managing to tame each strand into submission despite regrowth.

It was soon Wednesday and Brenda had arranged to meet Amma. Veronica was relieved when she appeared ready, without the hair gel.

'Where are you two off to?'

'Not sure. Amms should be here any minute.'

The door bell rang and CJ and Amma fought to hug her first.

'Where we goin', girl?'

'Dunno. It's your manor.'

'Hear ar nuh?' Amma mimicked. They all laughed including Veronica who now stood in the doorway enjoying them.

'I need to go to the passport office but I haven't even got the form yet.'

'Okay, we can get that at the Post Office on the High Road, and move on from there.'

Brenda turned to Veronica. 'I'll get some photos done now and we can fill in the form later, yeah?'

'We can go passport office tomorrow, Brends, you need company on dem missions. Das all day business. Man, I neva forget I went on me own when I got mine,' CJ announced.

'Did you get it same time?'

'Yeah, I had to go quick for me granny's funeral innit.'

'What else d'you need?'

'I fink jus' your birth certificate an' the old passport.'

'I thought you said that trip wasn't until next year. I can post off for your passport,' Veronica interrupted.

'I need proof of a valid passport and a deposit the day after I go back, otherwise I can't go. I might as well sort it while I'm down. If you get my birth certificate then we're fixed.'

'Okay. Come we goh,' Amma said, ready.

Veronica said goodbye, then turned closing the door on their excitement. Aunt B's words visited her: 'Yuh wi mess up de pikini' ed.' For a short while life had seemed at last to float on the past instead of being weighed down by it. Faced now with a problem neither love nor money could solve, Veronica wondered how she had let this happen.

GUITAR
Jamika Ajalon

Jimi took the fugitive express
his chariot glistened and
burst with an ease
that could erase time

I was trying to paint your picture. For days. Resistance.
I propped it against the tin cup you gave me. The photo
was smudged with various colours in one corner.
Eyes insistent you stared back at me. I had distanced
myself from you. You knew it. I lost a sense of
cohesion, paintbrush balanced pointlessly on the edge
of an old Nescafé jar. A dusty canvas stood ripped and
scorned with splashes of oils I am still trying to get off
blue hands.

I thought it was the machine that woke me up. An
abstract message. One screaming strum on your brand-
new, second-hand guitar. I wiped sleep from my
eyes. Lifting myself up from the too-soft sofa, I walked
back over to the easel. As I picked up the picture the
morning light filled in the crevices of the time-worn tin

cup. We found it during one of our street-roaming sessions, right outside some British Rail station. We decided to hang and roll a spliff. There was no one on the platform but us – too late for trains. As a joke we put the tin cup out for spare change from the universe.

Your fingers instantly found the chords releasing these lyrics from my chest.

> *here I go again,*
> *I've seen this place before*
> *here I go again ...*

I put the picture back against the tin cup. I had to break the cycle. You gave me this picture the day I came over geared up to tell you that I needed a change. Space. The words slept in my throat. Had to move on. Could you come with me?

I opened the window overlooking the lone patch of scrubby grey grass in the middle of the estate. An older man walked in pace with the slow heat unusual for London. Every leaf falling, bird flying, ladybird crawling, moved like molasses. I left the cubicle that was my room kicking stones in my head. I started walking and sank into the scenery: the driving, crying, hustling, addicts dropping, graffiti tattoos singing a blues. I was talking to myself, rehearsing my lines. What I would say when I saw you.

Mumbling out loud is not an absurdity on Brixton's front line, but of course someone had to respond. Even though it was obvious I wasn't talking to him an Adidas-clad brother had to come out with some silly shit like 'Why don't you smile my Nubian queen?' as if what he had in his pockets would win a grin. I continued the conversation I was having with myself and walked on. Further down the road, a dog-on-string beggar without the dog interrupted my train of thought. He looked like he may have surfed the rock and roll trip one time too many.

'Hello African goddess, can you spare some change?'

I cringed. African goddess? Nubian queen? I felt as if I were some spiritual Rasta pasta for the hungry. Normally I would have said sorry mate at least, but an inherited reaction kicked in. Protecting my teats, I walked on ignoring him.

Reaching the end of the lane I ran into the Wolf, or rather I heard him first, finishing off his kerbside concert with a defiant strum and gravelly lyric. Members of his posse, including a few half-interested bystanders, gave him his props, passing him a well-earned Kestrel. Normally Wolf would have stopped me, first accusing me (sometimes rightly) of pretending not to see him. I would endure only long enough to enjoy breaking him down. The big bad Wolf silenced and panting.

Any other day you might have been there, sharing a Kestrel, in the midst of some beer-fuelled 'debate'. But you weren't. Your guitar was, however, slung over this wiry man's shoulder. As I walked past him my gaze settled on his weather-worked fingers – hands which bent chords into brash rhythms, poised comfortably on the six-string acoustic Yamaha. I stared hard, hoping my laser-eyes would burn. Wolf saw me, but said nothing. I kept going.

I followed a path worn through the lawn, careful of the dog-shit mines, which lay behind apparently innocent blades of grass. I jumped the low wall that winds around the stone mesh path to your building. As my boots hit the concrete, I saw a butterfly nestled in the stone wall, blending; tan and grey designs on its still wings. Was it resting or was it dead? The sun hit a rough metal pole bulging through the cement.

I stood for a moment, mesmerised. A tabby meowed lazily before leaping into the courtyard. Never sure if the buzzer was working, I followed her and banged on your window.

'Hey.' Ripe cherry lips curved underneath a shadow of a moustache.

'Ran into Wolf on the way here,' I said after a kiss hello on those lips.

Collapsing on the bed I began to rationalise away my original mission. I took pleasure in watching you. I would miss this too much. You walked carefully around the clutter covering your treasured skip-scavenged rug, and sat gracefully in front of the piano. Picking up a fag end off of a half coconut shell you made a small exasperated gesture.

'People just walk all over me,' you began. 'I don't know. Am I a matador? A . . . ?'

'. . . Mat at the door,' I chimed in.

You finished your fag, before positioning your hands above the piano keys. I settled in, preparing myself for your embellished rendition of a Chopin piece. I scanned the room; a comfortable deterioration saturated walls decorated with markered messages. A few old paintings from your past exhibitions were propped on shelves against walls, all around the front room. A Bob Marley photo hung above an out-of-date calendar, next to one of your paintings: a city centre. Nigeria. Every square inch busy with packed buses and colourful people: from a distance a wash of hues. You stopped mid-bar as you often did when practising.

'Want some coffee? I might even have a clean glass.'

'Imagine that.' I sat up and began a rollie. 'Yeah, I'll have one.'

'Did Wolf say anything?'

I looked in at you through a space where glass should have been in the door.

'What could he say?' I countered.

'Cream and sugar?' You shook a can of Carnation milk at me.

'Yeah – one sugar, no two.'

I lit up. The spoon clicked a measured pace as you stirred in the delicate balance of dairy and sweet, somehow making an instant taste like heaven. Everything you did was creation.

'Most of this mess happened last Tuesday...' You passed me a cup. 'Wolf begged me to let him borrow the guitar – '

'What happened to his?'

'He pawned it. Said he'd make the money back.'

'I can't believe you let him take it.' I laid back on the futon as you updated me on this latest drama. You always had a story for me; sometimes I was an eyewitness.

'I never go anywhere without my guitar. With it, people leave me alone. The police don't even bother me. It's protection.'

If you'd had your guitar with you when the police stopped us, I wonder, would they have let us go? That night we went out together on a mission to confront your real mother. She would never respond to your letters. You only knew that your father was Nigerian. It was the 1950s. She couldn't handle raising a black baby boy alone. She put you up for adoption.

In Chelsea. You clean shaven in suit and myself in jeans and leather cap; I held your hand outside her house. Perhaps we stood too long. Perhaps your mum saw you and decided to call the cops. Maybe she saw me and thought I would try to claim her as well.

'What are you doing there?' We didn't even hear the patrol car drive up.

You tried to make light a tense situation. 'We were just trying to catch up with the Joneses... This is the Joneses' residence?' You spoke a perfect Queen's English that seemed to startle and annoy the officer.

Her name was Catherine Jones. The police did not get or like the joke. Instead they found amusement attempting to twist your arm behind your back. Your first reaction was to free yourself from the unsolicited grip. This only attracted more unwanted attention; now there were two of them grabbing and pushing you down.

It was like a scene from *EastEnders*. Head twisting towards Mrs Jones's front door, you stopped struggling long enough to yell, 'Mum, tell them who I am!'

They fished through your wallet but never checked your ID.

'This is his mother's house.' I turned and pointed. I thought I saw a face duck behind the curtains.

'Yeah, right,' said one of the cops. 'We'll have none of your little boy games.' He held me against a wall, his fist in my chest, searching me with a free hand.

He found a wad of cash that this 'black boy' couldn't have possibly earned. You looked at me helplessly. As they marched us over to the car I told them they should have got a female officer to search me. He was about to reply, then it finally dawned on him; he reddened. You were charged with attempted breaking and entering.

Me, I was your accomplice.

'To Rah Jah Kipling.' You slammed your empty coffee mug down on the counter in the kitchen for emphasis. 'No guitar. No money. I can't keep my electricity on without my guitar. What am I gonna to do?'

Hesitating, I ventured, 'Paint?'

'*Paint?* I have no money for canvas, oils, and no space.' You slip-kicked a layer of newspapers in your rampage.

'Maybe you need to let go of your guitar. Maybe you don't need the prop any more, maybe it's a sign.' I swung my arms around as if presenting him with his flat and the state of it. 'This? It's not you. I mean I can't go through this with you any more...'

The debris cluttering your flat mapped out your decline. An archaeological dig would reveal much, each layer slated a slow disintegration. After so many years signing on it was as if you were wearing a badge that declared you unemployable. Main objective: survival.

'I can't watch you go through this any more,' I repeated, locking eyes with you.

Pause. You stared past me, as if I was somehow missing the point and slid something down from the top of the piano.

'I have something for you.'

You handed me an old photograph. A younger image, same spirit, perhaps less damaged, a nuance of you. One I longed to capture.

'But maybe you don't need it after all.' There was a slight chuckle edging these words.

The doorbell whined.

'Who is that now?'

You walked to the intercom. I heard some muffled voice before you returned to the front room.

'It's Wolf.'

'Shit. Why did you let him in?'

Shrugging your shoulders, 'Generous?'

'Listen, I've got to go.'

'Stay.' You played with the skin around your fingernail. 'You can talk to him.'

I didn't move. 'I am not your mother' strained behind bars of clenched teeth, but instead I asked again, 'Why are you letting him in?'

'The guitar,' head down you whispered. 'Without it I don't exist.'

That was no answer.

You folded your arms and smiled. 'I am a disappearing act as we speak.'

I looked at you and waited.

Silence.

It took everything I had to say, 'I've got to go.' And mean it.

> *the truth is left to die*
> *the phrophets*
> *they lament*
> *'cos there's no tears left to cry*
> *i'm just sittin' on this stoop*
> *being myself waiting on the east wind*
> *love is all that's left*

I was trying to paint your picture. For days. Resistance. I propped it against the tin cup you gave me. The photo was smudged with various colours in one corner. Eyes insistent you stared back at me. I had distanced myself from you. You knew it.

A screaming guitar cut through my sleep. Piercing. Deep. I walked over to the easel and picked up your photo. The picture was fading.

I pedalled fast to your house; by the time I arrived only the eyes in the photograph remained lucid. The window was open so I jumped through. A shadow twisted into a crescent over the piano. From a gash, blood seeped over ivory keys. Above you, a self-portrait; stained sepia, propped on the music stand.

TAKE COURAGE
Krishna Dutta

1

A strange and susurrus sound woke her. She opened her eyes reluctantly to the glow of the bedside lamp. As she leaned across his body beside her to switch off the light she heard the noise again. It was the hopeless anguish of a trapped breath. He was in the throes of a massive heart attack. She jumped up, tripped a little and dialled the emergency number.

It was about 2 a.m. The oscillating light of the waiting ambulance intermittently illuminated the thin blanket of snow outside, while the rest of the genteel London suburb remained wrapped in the cosy slumber of a December night. When one of the ambulance men waiting with a clipboard asked her in a subdued voice, 'What was the gentleman's name?', the impact of the event slowly began to dawn on her.

'His name was...' She paused for a while as she began to realise that from now on her husband, her lover for eighteen years, would have to be referred to in the past tense.

'So you left me like this! How could you?' she screamed, piercing the thick silence of the night.

The doctor quickly put his hand on her shoulder and gently escorted her out of the bedroom into the living room downstairs. He then went into the kitchen and brought her a cup of tea. Imported from India, 'a cuppa' was the English cure for all maladies – a curious anomaly, Keya thought as she took a sip and relished its liquid warmth.

'I am very, very sorry, Mrs Das,' the doctor muttered, swaying his head in a gesture of woe. Keya, still holding the cup in her palms for residual warmth, desperately tried to figure out what it all meant to her: the night, the doctor in the house, Bimal's lifeless body upstairs and their seven-year-old daughter asleep in her room unaware of this momentous event in her life.

'Would you like me to ring your family in India, Mrs Das?' the doctor asked.

'Yes please, but can you call my cousin in Neasden first? The number is...' she recited it accurately from memory and went to the toilet upstairs. She did not return to the bedroom.

2

The day after the funeral, Keya took Nila to school and returned home alone. He was everywhere – the rooms flaunted all his earthly belongings mercilessly, each item with its intimate and precise smell, shape and place of its own. A feeling of vulnerability began to germinate inside her. She shed her duffle coat and slumped on the sofa. The grey morning outside tempted a paralytic torpor. Would she give in? She craved the way he teased her about being lazy, the way he would say *khukumoni* –

'little darling' – when she used to curl up in her favourite foetal position on the settee, his untranslatable Bengali compliments on her lissom and nimble body. He would run fingers through her tangled tresses, stroke her toes. She would tap on his lips with her index finger. He would bite it.

Keya remembered the first time they met. He was the editor of a small literary journal with offices in North Calcutta, and had asked Keya to come in and meet him. He had a reputation as one of the more rigorous and exacting editors; and when she had submitted an erotic love poem, part of her instinctively knew it would catch his attention. When she introduced herself, he appeared a little surprised. He tried to look placid and distant yet several times Keya felt his eyes stray searchingly onto her face – intrigued, she felt, to find the author of such a passionate piece to be this demure girl.

'Who is your favourite Bengali poet, *other* than Tagore?' he asked her. 'Vidyapati,' she remembered replying promptly, pleased that she was ready with such a substantial alternative. He would not mention Vidyapati again to her until they made love many months later. He bought her an old edition from the railings of College Street in Calcutta. He would often hum *kirton* after making love. His tenor voice would waft around the room, enveloping her in a delicious trance. The subtle erotic nuances of Vidyapati's Brajobuli verse, when sung properly, made it the most appropriate music for tender physical intimacy, even in a foreign environment.

He primed her for everything. They moved to England together within a year of their love-marriage. Instead of letting her join him later as was usually the custom, he made sure that they made the journey together. He encouraged her to take up further studies, to read good books, to attend quality shows, exhibitions, cinemas, concerts and performances. He supported her when she reluctantly decided to give up wearing saris and tried western clothes for battling with the British weather.

Would she be able to survive without his constant attentive companionship? Would she be able to stay and bring up Nila in England? Could she? The doorbell chimed – yet another bouquet.

'I do not need any more flowers!' she wanted to shout out to the Interflora messenger. Instead she accepted them with a sad smile, tipped him and left them in the hallway. She went into the kitchen and vaguely groped for something to eat. Most of the stuff in the fridge was too old, so she chucked it out and decided to go shopping. But he was no longer there to drive her to the supermarket and suddenly the shops seemed a fair way off by public transport. Again a gnawing feeling of helplessness ran through her veins. She must fight it. She must not succumb. She must get out of the house at once. She picked up her duffle coat and the house keys, checked her purse and headed for the bus stop. The cold truth that she would no longer have the privacy of a warm car unless she learnt to drive gave her a certain sense of purpose. She would have to learn to drive.

3

On Nila's eighth birthday there was a definite feeling of spring in the air. Keya decided not to have a party at home. She had invited six of Nila's selected friends to the local McDonald's for a treat. For the past five months Keya had tried her best to keep Nila's routine as normal as possible. A child needs the security of a regular pattern in life.

Keya had worried that Nila would not recover from the shock of her father's absence, so she had deliberately cultivated close contacts with friends who were single mothers. Together they went swimming, to ballet lessons, garden fêtes, museums, pantomimes and trips. Privately between the two of them, they never stopped talking about 'Daddy'.

'Do you remember what Daddy used to say whenever he drove past McDonald's?' asked Nila on her way back from the party.

'You remind me,' replied Keya tactfully.

'Need to stop for a wee pee,' imitated Nila in her father's voice.

They both laughed and Keya felt reassured in the knowledge that their daughter had inherited his sense of humour. This legacy would shield her in years to come.

She recalled one October evening when they had had to abandon their car in fog and walk home to Hampstead. All the way he entertained her with an imaginary conversation between Holmes and Watson as two Bollywood detectives in search of a missing prophylactic amulet for sexual prowess.

'My dear Watson, the couple in the painting on the victim's bedroom wall are practising the sixty-fourth position of the *Kama Sutra*,' he would utter in a crisp upper-class voice. He was a natural mimic.

On this May afternoon she mourned him again deeply for those inimitable hilarious anecdotes and for the loss of that unique lightness of being she felt in his company. The reality of missing him on Nila's first birthday since his death was hard.

When they got home, she poured two glasses of orange juice. Nila appeared in the kitchen in her pyjamas, looking tired but content. They watched a video of

Bedknobs and Broomsticks for a while. Soon it was Nila's bedtime, when Keya would tuck her up and say: 'Good night, sleep tight.'

'Wake up bright in the morning light,' Nila would complete the mantra. Keya had forgotten when this bedtime ritual began. Habit continued as ever – although the third voice was noticeably absent.

The ritual of putting Nila to bed propelled Keya back into the past. This was the time when Keya and Bimal would go downstairs together – have a drink, talk, listen to music, watch TV or just unwind with a book. As a couple they were a self-contained unit: secure in each other's company, they did not have the urge to cultivate close friendships with anyone else.

The friends they did have were broadly split into two distinct and invariably separate groups. The majority of their Bengali friends were preoccupied with living away from home and did not find much time for books and culture. Their English acquaintances on the other hand were vaguely interested yet ill-informed about India, though they were good at introducing them to the English mores and milieu. However, among such incompatible acquaintances, they did manage to find intellectual stimulation in the thoughts and ideas of writers, painters, filmmakers and musicians. Socially they would attend weekend get-togethers in Belsize Park or Notting Hill where professional Bengalis thronged in the sixties and seventies. At these *addas* – or gatherings – Keya would savour traditional prawn curries cooked by veteran housewives, with authentic ingredients bought from musty greengrocers in Drummond Street. They would listen to a variety of Bengali music, including Tagore's, and pick up useful information about the sales and bargains in the shops. At one such *adda* she heard about a Bengali law student who turned up at a party with a caged bird from a pet shop. Years later she would still tease him for literally bringing along 'a bottle and a bird' – in this case a parakeet from Harrods – just like it said to on the invitation! Bimal did not care much for such parties, but when he was there, he would become the life and soul of the gathering, with his talent for singing and sharp wit.

Their English friends would invite them to buffet suppers in Islington or Greenwich. Subdued light, candles on the table, muted Ravi Shankar–André Previn on the music centre, the smell of incense floating around hushed voices, created a romantic ambience. They would sit there together, squeezing each other's hands – a shy contrast to the other couples who were far more openly demonstrative. They would meet new faces while pecking at melon cubes wrapped in ham on a cocktail stick, sipping Spanish wine. They would discuss the latest William Blake exhibition at the Tate. Bimal would comment on Blake's political imagery and his inclusion of personalities like Pitt and Nelson in his paintings – much to the guests' surprise. Keya, draped in a silk sari, would secretly enjoy the admiring glances from other men, bemused by their studious interest in 'the Indian couple' and their precious manner towards her.

4

Keya went back into the back bedroom. It used to be his study. She found paperwork therapeutic. She sat on his chair and absorbed herself in replying to a solicitor's note, writing reassuring replies to her family in Calcutta about her and Nila's well-being in a so-called alien and allegedly racist country. She then started work on preparing lesson plans for the following day's teaching. All this took her late into the night. Finally, thoroughly exhausted, she shuffled to her side of the double bed and dived into an instant sleep. She had always been a good sleeper, now she was thankful for it.

The persistent trace of tobacco on his belongings was like invisible poisoned gossamer. The smell transported Keya to the days when he was very much alive. The aroma of cigarettes would hang around him. At times when he made love to her, smelling strongly of recent smoke, she would tenderly but almost unconsciously push his face slightly away from her nostrils. He would become instantly apologetic and she would always forgive him easily. Now she regretted that forgiveness.

Many years ago they walked through the unlit, swarming streets of Calcutta. They were returning from watching Polanski's latest movie, *Knife in the Water*. He was fascinated by its theme of a generation in conflict. Through the din and babble of Chowrangee Road they talked incessantly about the Bengali middle class's obsession with conformity. A doctor's son must become a doctor. A college-educated daughter should marry 'upwards' into affluence.

He was a part-time schoolteacher and the literary journal didn't pay much; she a university student. They decided to marry and travel to Europe. England, in particular, had nourished their romanticism, aroused their intellectual curiosity and fuelled their hopes of meeting like-minded people. After all they were from Calcutta, where the East truly met the West. So they planned and saw the officials at the British Council. And many months later, one bright April afternoon in 1969, they arrived at London's Victoria Station. A lone Bengali friend waited to greet them with a bunch of bright yellow daffodils. Fair daffodils, Keya thought, what a suitable welcome. Ever since she had read Wordsworth's poem in her school days she had longed to see the real flower.

In the taxi Keya silently wondered about a new life in a new country. Their friend took them to a small room on the second floor of a tall house beside a quiet and empty street.

'This area is quite central. The British Museum is only fifteen minutes' walk away. The rent is affordable and the landlord is a Bengali,' he informed them. 'And, as you have a work permit, finding a suitable job won't be difficult.'

Keya still recalled the room vividly. It had two draughty sash windows overlooking the street, a very high ceiling with a pendant light, a hand basin in the corner with a cupboard underneath and a twin gas ring with a saucepan and an aluminium kettle. It was a total contrast from their sprawling family home in Calcutta, which had three inner courtyards, a maze of verandas, corridors and rooms with dark stairways leading to huge flat rooftops with wrought iron railings. Yet Keya did not feel nostalgic. On the contrary, she liked the compactness of the bedsit. She looked forward to their time together in that neat room, with no peeping servants, no insensitive relatives and no 'do's and don'ts' for a young wife in an extended family of some renown.

Once they were alone they danced a silent waltz, moving between the well-worn coffee table and the bed that was covered in a powder-green candlewick spread. Bimal said: 'We must get hold of a second-hand record player as soon as we can afford one,' and skilfully hummed the opening notes from Mozart's allegro of 'Eine Kleine Nachtmusik'. She agreed.

5

Now Keya woke up to the cold and distanced patter of Radio 4. She missed rising languidly to the sound of his living presence around the house. He was always up before her and the warm, soapy, intimate smell in the bathroom after he had used it was a luxury she looked forward to in winter. She buried her face in the flannel and wept silently. Hearing Nila stir, she composed herself, put on her glad voice and called out, 'Good morning, sweetheart.'

'Morning, Mum.'

'It's a lovely morning and I'm going to give my lovely baby a kiss and a cuddle.'

'I'm not a baby. I'm eight,' she protested. 'I have a birthday present from Daddy,' Nila mysteriously announced.

'Have you?' Keya asked, trying not to sound disconcerted.

'Look at the window, Mum.'

Keya turned to the window but could not see anything unusual.

'Can't you see something red?' Nila persisted.

Keya noticed the spindly and abandoned pot of geraniums that had been left on the window sill since last autumn – one had suddenly bloomed into a bright scarlet flower. A child's imaginary gift from a missing father. Simultaneously she felt delighted at Nila's resourcefulness in coping with her own grief and fearful that her daughter would continue to believe in his disembodied presence.

On the way to school Keya intentionally pointed to the trees in the park – after a long, harsh winter they had finally blossomed. They talked about springtime when nature wakes up and procreates. At the school gate Keya kissed Nila on the cheek as they parted. Nila ran towards a group of children milling around in their blue and grey uniforms and instantly became one of them – absorbed into the mass.

6

For a while now Keya had been feeling somewhat restless. Although she had established a new rhythm in her life around work and Nila, so far she had been unable to settle down to any serious pursuit. She had not read a book for a good while. She had not listened to her favourite music since his death. The memory of sharing such interests was still raw inside her. Occasionally she would dust the books in the study, fondly take one off the shelf and leaf through it. Overcome with sadness she would hold it close to her while her mind wandered off into the recesses of unbidden association.

Some years ago, they had journeyed to Hay-on-Wye one late July morning. The allure of bookshops stuffed to the ceiling with obsolescent printed tomes was irresistible. Many years' experience of looking out for good books among trash along the temporary stalls outside Presidency College in Calcutta had made Bimal the skilled bibliophile that he was. He soon managed to befriend a few old pros, who ushered them into their darker and dustier basements for more timeworn moth-eaten delights. He filled the car boot to capacity. Keya had bought just one book. A gold-embossed, hand-bound, early edition of *Tales from Shakespeare* by Charles and Mary Lamb.

When she was small Keya's father used to retell Shakespeare's stories in Bengali with great gusto. She and her younger brother and sister would listen spellbound throughout, imagining the events as told with Indian images and brown-skinned characters. Their father would modulate his voice dramatically to whisper the mesmerising tune of Ariel – the benign incorporeal *bhut* uttering:

> Fuul faathoom fiive thi faatheerr llies
> Ov hes boones arr coorralls maade
> Thoosse arr parrls thaatt weerre hes eiess . . .

As the monsoon rain whipped the window's old wooden shutters, a dimly lit room in Calcutta would be transformed into the stormy desert island of Prospero and Miranda.

Keya decided to find her mislaid copy of the tales. It was about time she introduced Shakespeare to Nila.

7

Keya had been thinking of visiting relatives in Calcutta. She knew she had to do it as a part of her grieving process. Now she was ready to meet the family as herself and as Nila's protector – not just as a helpless heartbroken widow. She had saved up enough for their passage. The time seemed right for the trip to India.

Keya arrived at Mrs Sterling's to pick up Nila. She was wheeling a small wheelbarrow full of dead flower heads in the garden, while Mrs Sterling was kneeling down, head bent among the pile of garden refuse. She spotted Keya and called out: 'Come in, dear. It's time for a tea-break.'

'Can we have a picnic in the back garden, Aunty-Mummy?' Nila asked.

'Yes, of course, but it'll have to be a "pick-tea". I only have a packet of biscuits to offer.'

'Picnic-ticnic as we would say in Bengali,' Keya butted in.

'Marigold-Terry-gold,' whispered Nila into Mrs Sterling's ear.

'You rascal! You've seen my box of chocolates! Oh, well, I suppose we'll have some of them too.'

They laughed and went inside.

Nila had a slice of shortbread between her teeth. Mrs Sterling pushed the power switch of the kettle and waited for it to gurgle while getting the tea tray ready for the garden. Keya pulled out three garden chairs from the shed and placed them in an intimate set under the pear tree. It was June, and the faint yet savoury aroma of thyme wafted up from the small herb patch nearby.

After tea, Nila asked, 'Can I go inside and watch *Blue Peter*?'

'Yes, love.'

Nila ran indoors. The cat sauntered after her in pursuit of better prospects.

'I wonder how Nila will react to Calcutta,' Keya mused.

'She seems excited. She was showing off her knowledge of Bengali before you came. *Beerraal* – cat, she taught me.'

Keya smiled indulgently at her ill-accented pronunciation of the word and said, 'She'll cope with the language, I know, and she'll pick up more over there. I am thinking more about the place and the people.'

'Children are pretty resilient creatures, my dear. You'll be surprised how quickly they adjust. She'll have a lot of attention too and that'll help.'

'You see, we lead a simple and quiet life here. Over there it'll be all lavish and loud with servants and well-off relatives fussing unnecessarily. They will want to pamper us. Nila might feel confused.'

'Well, you are going there for a holiday. Holidays are always lavish.'

'It is not a holiday for me. It is obligatory. We've only just begun to live with grief behind us. There it'll start all over again as soon as we get to the airport, with tears, sighs and wails. I am dreading it.'

'Have you talked about it to Nila?'

'No. Not yet.'

'You should. You need to prepare her.'

'Can you help me?'

'Of course I will if you want me to, but you'll have to make the start in your own time.' Mrs Sterling put her hand softly on Keya's shoulder. She sat there in the blossoming brightness of the garden with an idle gaze while images of her married home in Calcutta flitted through her mind. Familiar faces interspersed with memories of the torrential monsoon that clogged the drains and magically turned the city into Venice in a couple of hours. Silently she let the images multiply.

Since Keya had announced her trip to India, the question she had to answer most was:

'Are you returning for good?'

Today Nila came back from school and asked the same.

'No. We are going there for five weeks during the holidays and you'll be back before school opens again.'

'I thought so too.'

'We are going there to let Grandma see that we are all right. We are doing fine. She needs to know that. Do you understand?'

'She'll miss Daddy.'

'Yes, everyone there will miss him and you and I will have to show them that we are well. That we are trying to look after ourselves without Daddy as well as we can. That will make them feel better.'

'We are not going to live in India for ever and ever, are we?' asked Nila, anxiously.

'No we are coming back.'

'That's not what my teacher thinks.'

'I will write a note to your teacher tomorrow,' Keya said, firmly.

'Will we still live in this house when we come back?'

'And why do you think we won't?'

''Cos Vicky's Mum was telling Liam's big sister...I heard.'

Keya suddenly became irritated. Why didn't people just mind their own business? Maybe they think I'm incapable of living here and bringing up Nila on my own. This is the only place in the world where I feel comfortable and secure. This is the only environment that will allow me to choose the kind of life I think is right for me. They would rather have me back in India among my own people because they think I need protection. She wished she could return to her life as it was before Bimal's unexpected death. Now everything was all messed up.

'Can we get Natalie's birthday present from India?' asked Nila, as if to be more certain of returning among her friends after the visit.

'We will. Would she like a mirrored skirt? Why don't you ask her?'

'I'd like one too.'

'You'll have to leave some space in your case to bring back presents and gifts,' said Keya, in a bid to reassure her further. To herself she whispered, 'Take courage. Take courage.'

When Keya first came to London, the slogan was plastered all over the place in neon; it caught her eye at almost every turn, 'Take Courage'. For some time she took the phrase to be some kind of a moral message to the citizens of England, similar to the Tagore quote of 'Walk Alone' scrawled on the back of many ramshackle Calcutta rickshaws. Daunted by the demands of living in an unfamiliar city, in moments of exasperation she would often mutter to herself 'Take Courage'. One summer evening, sipping lemonade in a cosy Hampstead pub, her eyes fell on a beer mat depicting the legend and she realised her mistake. It was a brand of stout. The comedy of it never failed to amuse her. However the habit of privately muttering the words in critical moments remained.

Keya picked up the day's mail and proceeded to open a parcel containing the Bengali journal they had been subscribing to for years. It was the first time she looked through its contents with interest for months. She began to read the opening section from a memoir of a housewife originally written around 1830. The simple narrative was earthy and engrossing. When Nila came in from the garden Keya was still absorbed in reading, so Nila silently picked up her copy of *Winnie the Pooh* and sat reading beside her mother. At that moment the familiar corner of the living room witnessed the beginning of a small but significant affair. They read on till the grey afternoon outside turned into an unexpectedly clear moonlit evening with a starry sky.

Over dinner, Nila asked: 'Daddy did like *Winnie the Pooh*, didn't he?'

'I think he did.'

'When you burnt the cake one day I remember he called it Crustimoney Proseedcake. That's a Pooh word for Customary Procedure. I read it today.'

'I am glad that you still remembered it,' responded Keya.

After supper, while washing up, Keya unconsciously began humming a meditative song by Tagore:

> *If I am starved of love*
> *Why then is the dawn sky infused with*
> *Such rousing melodies?*

She sang the entire song to herself and once more appreciated the genius of the poet who achieved a rare union between spoken words and delicate notes. She felt better. Sitting on the stairs Nila listened quietly and asked afterwards, 'Can you teach me this song, Mum?'

'Maybe when you are a bit older.'

'Aren't there some easy ones?'

'Yes there are. Children in the poet's school sing them all the time. I'll get some tapes for you. You can listen and may even learn to hum the tunes.'

'When we go to India will you take me to visit the poet's school?'

'Yes, if you want to.'

'I would love to. What is it like?'

'Sometimes they have lessons outdoors under a tree.'

'That must be fun. Can I take some photos to bring back?'

'Yes, but now let's go to bed and I'll tell you a story that my daddy used to tell me when I was little.'

'What's it about?'

'It's about a magical island where a little girl lived with her father, until one day a ship wrecked there and . . .'

RED SARI
Amanthi Harris

I first saw the dress in a magazine for brides-to-be; the bride in the picture was small and young, and she had dark curly hair, like me. She was standing on a stone, in a stream, lifting the ivory dress just above the water, above the white satin shoes on her feet. A dark wood rose up behind her, green and blurred, but a band of sun fell across her face, on her golden cheeks, and she smiled in it, her eyes far away. In the wood, in the stream, in her floating ivory dress, she looked like me and I wanted to be her, for her to be me.

'But a dress!' my mother exclaimed when I finally brought it up. 'How can you wear a dress? You must wear a sari.' And she added: 'Don't you think?'

A distant little voice in me agreed, a distant me nodded. 'Yes, a sari; I'll have to try one on.'

'You will look lovely in a sari,' my mother said, and I began to think that maybe I would. I wondered what Andrew would think, if he would know what to think, and I tried to see how I might look coming down the aisle, or whatever there was at a registry, and all I saw was the woodland scene and a cloudy sky, and myself stamping through the wet grass, away from it. And the woman stayed with the stream, unseeing, uncaring that I was leaving; smiling to herself. She grew smaller, smaller, became an ivory glimmer through the dark ribs of trees. But however far I walked she did not disappear, or maybe I was lingering really, not going away, watching her, seeing her smiling face.

Winter arrived and I went with my mother to look at saris and jewellery for weddings, to a part of town like a town in India, but with Debenhams and Argos, and Tesco and an Iceland. Squat men walked hunched through the streets, jackets zipped to their chins, and women pushed prams, carried shopping, held umbrellas up against the December drizzle. Old women tottered in sandals and woollen socks, duffle coats tight over sari frills that splashed with rain and mud from the pavement. Among them my mother and I walked, damp clinging to us, a dark grey sky unshifting above. We were headed for a sari shop that was recommended by someone my mother knew, but we stopped first at a canteen selling bhajis, puris, samosas, jellabies and even the rose-pink faluda drink that had been her favourite once.

'They have everything here now,' my mother observed.

We went around the counter and chose and sat down to eat, but it seemed strange to have no air conditioning, no sun outside, no squall of horns, no roar of traffic, no coconut trees against a blue sky above the shops. The faluda frothed in her glass, bubbled pink from the red jelly sweetness at the bottom. I almost saw her then, in cafés in Colombo with her cousins and friends, and how she and I might have been able to talk together as she had with them. She sat now, looking around her at the people in the canteen, looking them over carefully, table after table. And the people looked at us, wondering perhaps just as my mother was, who we were, where we came from exactly, if we were the same as them, the same specific kind. I sucked on my straw and the red jelly strands wriggled in a rose-flavoured drift into my mouth.

I looked out of the window, and back at my mother, glared at the back of her hair, but not for long in case she turned and caught me, saw the mutiny I felt, saw how all I wanted was to get up and run away, get on the train back to where I lived. Outside the window, women strolled past; mothers, grown-up daughters with their babies and children, all laughing, talking, shopping together. Did they ever sit like us? I wondered. With nothing to say? The women laughed even though it was still raining and the sky was grey; I watched them and sucked the last pink foam of faluda in. Then I turned and watched the families inside, watched them all squeezed together in the nailed-down plastic chairs, bangles jingling on the edges of the metal plates. Babies waved food in the air. My mother finished eating, wiped her fingers in a serviette.

'Are you ready to go?' she asked and wrapped her scarf around her, put her coat on again.

We went first to a jeweller whom my mother knew. The jeweller was behind the counter with a crowd of busy women and men.

'These are his lovely sisters,' my mother said to me in her public cheerful voice, beaming at the women. They smiled at her and she smiled and smiled.

'This is my daughter,' she said to the jeweller. 'She is getting married.'

'Oh?' The man grinned at me.

The crowd of his sisters and their husbands behind the

counter lifted necklaces and satin trays of rings from beneath the glass. Necks and arms thrust forward for the rings and chains with ruby pendants, diamonds or sapphires to be twisted on or hung from. There was advice and discussion; mirrors held up, heads turned this way and that. The jeweller and his sisters and their husbands conferred together, all making suggestions. The men punched figures into Casio pocket calculators, shouted percentages, gave Special Discounts as Special Favours to Trusted Customers.

My mother paused before a pair of earrings and a necklace, her finger was poised on the glass pointing at them.

'Twenty-four carat gold, madam, nothing less,' said the jeweller coming over, his smile lifting up the edges of his glossy pelt. My mother pondered the necklace, held the chain of heavy links.

'We'll have to buy you the necklace, I suppose,' she said to me. 'He won't know about our customs after all. *There*, of course, the groom would buy the necklace himself.'

Andrew knew about it, I told her, and anyway I didn't want that particular necklace.

'There's no point him getting you cheap jewellery,' my mother said. 'You can't wear cheap jewellery for your wedding.'

I picked up one of the earrings, felt it surprisingly heavy in my hand. It turned out not to fit.

'Don't you wear earrings?' the jeweller demanded. He squinted at my ears.

'When you are married,' he said, 'you will be wearing good jewellery – these holes in your ears are not big enough. You will have to make them bigger. Here – I'll do it – '

He picked up the earrings and leaned over the counter towards me.

'I'll just push these in,' he said. 'It will only hurt a little.'

Diamonds sparkled in his hand as he darted forward. I yelped and jumped back before he got me, stood shocked before him and my mother because for a moment I had wanted to let him do it, let him tear my ear for all the heavy gold that I would never wear, to all the community events and family occasions that I never went to any more. The jeweller slowly straightened, controlling his annoyance, giving my mother a sympathetic smile as he packed the earrings back into their display case and slid them under the glass of the counter once more. I saw my mother look away, '. . . to look at things for herself', she said with a small hurt laugh. We left the jewellery shop shortly afterwards, and I promised, feeling guilty and relieved to be going, to consider the necklace, and perhaps another pair of earrings. We'd be back soon, we said.

We went away, down the road to a shop scented with jasmine incense, a shop draped in coloured silk. Purple, pink and green, gold-threaded cloth lined the room, pleated and pinned into fans along the walls. Women glided about inside, draping, folding, throwing open arms hung with glittering silks for customers to observe.

'Bridal,' my mother said to a red-lipped woman with pale, pitted cheeks.

At once, a shining pile of white and gold appeared, and I was rolled inside a stiffened sheath of stars and sprays of golden flowers. A group of women gathered around to watch.

'Lovely,' they all cried, a chorus.

I stared, encased, at my reflection.

'I don't think it's me,' I heard myself say, and the women looked at my face. At first they looked bemused, then I saw their eyes harden.

'You'll get used to it,' my mother said quickly, but she was frowning, and her lips were clenched thin.

'It's not me,' I protested, dismayed. 'I look shapeless.'

My mother gave a small taut laugh. 'That's only for now,' she retorted. 'I'll pleat it,' she said, 'and tuck it in tight on the day.'

But I heard the little stream, so distant now, and there was the woodland and the woman in her light pale shift smiling and humming to herself in the cool of the trees.

'I can't wear this,' I said.

My mother turned to the chorus and rolled her eyes.

'It's not me,' I said to her. The women looked at me and seemed to be waiting, as if more was needed as explanation. 'I don't like it,' I said, and a particular type of pause, of something final, settled between us all.

'This is what happens,' my mother sighed. She shook her head.

The women watched her, listened, breathing softly, their eyes expectant.

'Back home they would not argue, no?' my mother said.

The women nodded. They did not look at me, only glanced away, and then at each other. I caught the eye of one who seemed to be the youngest; I caught her just as she was staring into my face as if I was something she had never seen. I glared at her and at all of them. Couldn't they see what I looked like? I didn't look right. How could I get married looking like that?

The pitted-cheeked woman's red lips pursed, 'You should try to please your mother, no?'

Outside it grew dark. Streetlights cast a synthetic

orange light over the street, the orange of jelly before it is set. The weekend rolled into night. The black roads with their jelly light filled with cars packed with shopping bags and children wrapped warm, going home to *Stars in Their Eyes*, perhaps, as I had once to Beadle and Noel, and burgers and chips, and curry and rice and pickles especially imported for parents and aunts and uncles who might drop by in the evening, and fill up the house, keeping the black night world outside.

Inside the sari shop, the women turned the sign to 'Closed', counted money in the till, folded saris and put them away in a clamour of bangles – their own saris swishing as they fled around the room, locking up display cabinets and drawers.

'I know!' I cried, grasping a sari on a table. 'This one – I'll wear it to "go away" in – I'll wear a dress for the wedding, and a sari to "go away" in.'

My mother hesitated.

'You want to try on?' It was the woman with the red lips.

I nodded, and the sari unfolded – red and orange with gold borders – and cascaded a rich curtain around me. I emerged glowing red and gold and different now; turned to look at myself, revealed. The women paused to look at me, stayed looking, some smiled in the mirror at me and it felt like a reprieve.

'That suits you,' the woman with the red lips said. Her eyes softened. 'It suits you more than the first one,' she conceded.

My mother bought the red sari that day, but there was a blankness in her gaze as she paid, and an ache inside me as I saw the white and gold sari folded and put away.

I was married in the dress from the magazine; walked around all day with cool ivory silk against my skin, a silk veil and white chiffon floating behind me everywhere I went. And there were thin threads of silver in my ears, with opals that glowed in the sun, in candlelight, in streetlights in the taxi as we headed off at last, alone. The red sari I found years later, as I looked for a dress to wear to a wedding of friends, in a paper bag battered soft with age and moving house. I had never taken it out and my mother and I had never spoken of it again. I felt its plump red and gold folds. I could design a dress, I thought, a sari-dress, have it made. It would certainly be different, and perfect and mine. I would like it, I knew, just for that.

BREASTS
Donna Daley-Clarke

n. Milk-secreting organs of a woman; upper front part of human body, seat of affections.

My favourite newsreader is on the telly, wearing a blouse I can almost see through. I'm having breakfast in bed; half a carton of last night's chicken chow mein with a mug of tea made with an unused teabag and milk that doesn't smell bad even though the sell-by date passed two days ago. Good days start this way.

But there's traffic in my head.

Yesterday I came back from a five-a-side game and instead of the stench of cats and pilchards from Flat B, I smelt the instant-headache perfume worn by women who get on the 38 buses at West End stops. I took the stairs two at a time. A stringy blonde sat leaning against my bedsit door, leaving grease marks on my letters as she shuffled my post and ate a wedge of Domino's pizza.

'Can I help you?' I asked, trying to sound like one of those store detectives who are always up my arse, trying to be helpful.

She put down a crust with half a slice of pepperoni.

'Hi,' she said, extending an oily hand that I ignored. 'I work for the *Mail on Sunday*. Your dad's being released next week and the incident with your mum . . . well your version hasn't been told.' She pulled a sad face like a daytime telly presenter switching to world disasters after recipe of the week.

'Nah, I'll pass,' I said, snatching my post from her hand. I put my key in the lock but I couldn't find the keyhole and the metal kept scratching.

'You're looking at fifteen thousand pounds,' she said.

'*You're* looking at concussion if you don't move.' I slammed the door, plugged in the hoover and upped the volume on the telly, but I still imagined owning a Saab 900 with a walnut wood interior and a wallpapered flat with underfloor heating. Then I remembered Mum, who starched and ironed the clothes she gave to Oxfam and I figured if I took the money I'd paint the walls yellow to hide the damp and then I could give this room to someone less fortunate. It would be perfect for a cripple. He could make himself a cup of tea in the breakfast bar without getting out of bed.

If I planned on lying, I would tell you my fifteen grand story happened on an ordinary summer's day – because it sounds more believable, and what you say stands out, like those black-and-white movies with a splash of red. But there was nothing normal about the summer of '76. The clay at the bottom of the River Lea cracked. Old people dried up and faded away and buses sat steaming in rush-hour traffic.

Given a choice I'd rather not think about that summer, or the money, but it's like the shred of chicken from last

night's chow mein trapped between my two front teeth
– it's just there.

I kept one of the newspaper articles about my biological
father. In the picture he has the square dimpled jaw I told
myself belonged only to Clint Eastwood and me. He
should be ugly. If evil were ugly we'd all know what we
were up against.

The reports differ: it was an accident, he has learnt to
control his anger, he was a promising football player.
(They leave out the banana throwing that had him sitting
on the bench at Crystal Palace until he transferred to the
sugar machine at Trebor.) The reports are all the same: he
is *sorry*. A word I use if I tread on a person's toe, or leave
a coffee ring on Auntie Harriet's table.

I'm gonna leave the newspaper with his picture in
outside Flat B. Maybe Nutty Suzy will use it for her cat
trays.

I cut a picture of Mum from the *Daily Express*. She is
a young girl in a hairy coat on the platform of Liverpool
Street Station. Boxes and a suitcase hide her feet. She is
standing next to a ticket collector; the zigzag ribbons in
her cornrowed hair level with the peak of his cap. She
runs from the top to the bottom of the photo like a
streak of golden syrup. I stuck her on the fridge so I see
her when I make tea. I had to move her from the wall
opposite my bed because I looked at her until she was all
blurry and I was all cut up, thinking of the extra years we
would have had if I'd known her before she was my
mum, when she was a girl.

Lately I've felt like an old biddy on *The Antiques
Roadshow* who has just been told her ugly jumble-sale
painting in the attic is worth half a million. I tried talking

to Auntie Harriet but she said, 'Geoffhurst, boy, you don't know jack.'

But I remember it all. Back to when my biological father was my dad. Saturday mornings with Hulk, sucking cola-cubes till the roof of my mouth bled, chewing black jacks till my gums were as black as my arse.

I need to go that far back because that's where one story starts and another ends.

They called me a liar last time. Now I'm nine years older, but girls still look at me sideways when I say nice things about them. It's my lazy eye; it gets in the way of the truth. If I were talking to you now I'd be looking straight at you but after a while my right eye would go off on its own. No one has believed me for as far back as I remember, and I put that down to my lazy eye.

Check this bloke on the telly. I knew something was up before he spoke because despite the rich white-boy suit (black wool, cut close, just short of tight) he's wearing navy socks. Turns out he doesn't know his wife's name or how many kids he has. A helpline number for brain-injured people has just flashed and gone, too quickly for a normal person to remember where he put his pen. I feel sorry for the poor bastard. I'd be happy to swap because he wants to remember, and I can't forget.

The summer of '76 was hot enough to wonder if government scientists were doing a weather experiment – inventing a fifth season or seeing if sunshine made you buy more soap.

The tar in the playground pulled away at my feet like a toffee strip. There were islands of vomit made by damp stinky kids who kept on playing and laughing in midday heat, kids called Sunbeam when they were nice, who had parents who told them to 'Turn the telly off and enjoy the sunshine.' After two terms of sucking up and one term of being reserve milk monitor, Shelly Springer finally got to be the real thing, and then they scrapped monitors because the milk kept curdling before eleven o'clock break. They moved playtime to quarter-past two when the sun had stopped blaring, but at half-past three, when school was out, we were still popping blisters on white girls' arms. The tune of the ice-cream van melted into traffic, and there were fights over stuff we would have been cracking up over a few months earlier. Craig tried to strangle Gordon with his tie for calling him a 'Sonovabeech', which Stuart had told Gordon was German for a tackle from behind.

The heat made my head move in and out. I forgot where the outside of my body ended so I kept getting bruises from door frames and table corners. I drank so much water, when I licked my arm I could taste dirt but no salt. My wee looked like cream soda, and I could piss my whole name against the wall and underline it, without running out. The kids who cycled from Sycamore Street were darker on their left sides where the sun hit them on their way home. Flies flew at half mast. Dogs stopped chasing cats.

It was the same summer I did a swap and Jason gave me what I thought were two *Spiderman* comics, but one was the *Incredible Hulk* and after a while Hulk filled up my head until I had to stop myself from squaring up to my Mum and saying, 'DON'T MAKE ME ANGRY; YOU WON'T LIKE ME WHEN I'M ANGRY.'

A few weeks after my introduction to Hulk my good eye noticed breasts.

I was cleaning the inside of my bedroom window after school, even though I could see out and sunlight saw in. I thought it was the sort of job women made up, which was why they didn't have time to invent cars or superheroes. Through the window I saw Theresa-Next-Door sunbathing on a blue-striped deckchair – her titties spread out like two fried eggs with overdone yolks. I didn't know she had them; she must have got them on Tuesday or Thursday. I can't be exact about that, but what I do know is she didn't have them the Saturday before.

That summer tits littered the park like conkers in October; they were pulled high in slings that tied at the neck, they pushed forward, swung loose or shoved up towards the faces of women who walked and talked normal, like they just didn't know.

The family breasts lacked stuffing. My sister's were gobstopper hard; even so I begged for a feel, in exchange for her turn on the washing-up rota, but once she knew how keen I was – though I tried to pretend I wasn't – she got silly and wanted me to be making her bed and all sorts. I could tell you my mum's tits were to my liking, but they weren't. They looked like flat bike tyres and the nipples gazed down at the floor in a sad search for a puncture repair kit.

I would have traded my *Supersurfer* collection for a pair of springy tits to keep in the box under my bed (with my milk tooth, a very long toenail clipping and an *Incredible Hulk* comic that I felt sure would one day earn me serious money).

I hoped tits would be like my bike that filled my head until I got it, and then it was no big deal and I was able to think about football again. I kept all this breast business to myself for the longest time, but now I come to remember, even in the infants, Wesley Sanders always had the back of his head nestled between Miss Blackwell's tits at story time.

Truth is, if I could go back to any time, I would choose being ten with a lazy eye, looking for breasts with lots of stuffing. And having a mother.

An edited extract from the novel *A Lazy Eye*

TRUSSED
Shiromi Pinto

—Vinda, Vinda, you're a—

   —Shut up, she hissed.

He trembled. His eyes rolled up, crossing in the effort to focus on the stiletto heel boring into his forehead. He let out a moan, knees cracking on laminate floorboards. —Feels good, doesn't it? she whispered. —Like a hard, cold, silver bullet.

She watched the rhythmic dilation and constriction of his belly button. Surrounded by copper hairs it flared over the edge of a white towel. —Nmmmm. Nmmmm. Nmmmm. He was whimpering in falsetto, joyous tears coursing down his cheeks. She removed her foot, sneering at the vague, trapezoidal hollow it left on his forehead. —Tell me I have a nice arse, she said, turning around and waving her buttocks at him.

He gazed at the slightly mottled brown flesh squeezing under the edge of her leather panties. —Oh...Oh. His eyes, wet with tears and perspiration, were lined red. —They're gorgeous. He grazed the underside of a cheek with his fingers.

—Don't touch, she screamed, snapping round to face him. —Did I say you could touch me? She leaned menacingly over his cowering body. —Did I? He knotted himself into a foetal tuck. —Answer me.

—N-n-no.

—Say you're sorry.

—I'm sorry.

—Louder.

—*I'm sorry*.

She patted his head with a gloved hand. —Naughty boy, she pouted, glancing quickly at her watch. It was a few minutes after ten-thirty. —And if naughty boy stays naughty, Vinda will be back. She grinned icily, peeling off her gloves.

He staggered towards the couch where his trousers lay, and fumbled through the pockets, extracting eighty-five pounds.

—I have to give you something. Something for… He shivered in his towel. She nodded, counting the money before folding it into her wallet.

Vinda sighed as she made her way towards Holborn tube, kit bag a pendulum hanging from her shoulder. She stared at the rubber lips of her blue suede trainers gleaming thick and white against the grey pavement. Every week she came to Bloomsbury to see Derek, the lawyer from Lincoln's Inn. He never acknowledged her if they caught one another's eye in Safeway or Harts. Then he was impeccable, if a little chubby, in his navy suit and wool–cashmere overcoat. But it was rare for Vinda to catch Derek in so dignified a costume. She was more accustomed to seeing him in a white towel, drawn around his body like an old-fashioned nappy. — Bloody lawyer, she muttered to herself. For all her time and effort, he never gave her more than eighty-five quid for the sixty minutes of pain she lavished on his chicken-skinned body. Still it was an undeclared supplement to her JSA bi-weekly cheques. Soon she would get a proper job, she promised herself, and start liking men again.

—He's the only guy I've ever met who gets off on my stretch marks. Vinda chewed on an apple as she spoke into the receiver. —Not only does he get off on them, he pays me for it too. Of course he's a pervert, so I can't say he gives me much hope. She laughed. —What a night, Am. How're you, anyway? How's the thesis going?

—Never mind the thesis, Vinda, I need a man.

Vinda rolled her eyes. —Oh God, not again.

—It's horrible, Amrik whimpered, —what do I do? I saw a stunning boy at the library today. I smiled. He smiled. I watched him go into the computer room, then followed him in. But when I got there he was chatting up some woman. What a waste.

Vinda surveyed her fingernails. They were short and blunt the way she liked them. —What're you doing tonight?

—I'm going to Russell Square. He sighed, —It's either that or King's Cross. Maybe I'll let some gross old man feel me up for money.

Vinda kissed her teeth. —Amrik, stop it. You're being silly. You know you can't get it up for the old men, anyway.

Amrik sniffed. —That's true. The last time I was offered money, I went with this old guy to the toilets, and nothing worked. I should have taken the money first, then at least I would have had twenty quid instead of cheap humiliation.

—Why do you do this to yourself? Vinda turned over onto her belly. She flicked at the edge of the quilt absently. —You deserve more than all these impersonal encounters.

—But when I need a man, I can't help myself.

—Sometimes it's better to wait until you get to know someone. I know you get frustrated. We all do. That's why we have hands and fingers.

—And hoovers. Amrik's voice was a barely audible whine. —You straight people don't understand. And anyway, his voice rose, —who are *you* to preach to me, madame? You spend half your evening whipping some poor sod and come home to dictate to me.

—Dictate? Who the hell is dictating? Vinda kicked a pillow off the bed. —And he isn't a poor sod, he's a bloody lawyer. He's loaded, and all he can spare is eighty-fucking-quid—

—Eighty quid! He gives you eighty quid! Amrik's words tumbled loudly through the receiver. —I get offered twenty if I'm lucky, and even that's not often.

—Get off it. This ain't no shake and stain, darling. What I do is art, nothing less. Like a geisha, you know. There's nothing trite about it.

Amrik took in a sharp breath. —Are you calling my sexual offerings trite? How dare you. I could just hang up.

—Stop playing the drama queen with me. Vinda rolled onto her back. —Anyway it's just Derek—

—For now—

—Shut up. I'm not a prostitute.

—One client is all it takes.

—Look, he's not a client, okay? I told you. He's sort of my boyfriend.

—Since when do boyfriends pay?

—In a more civilised world they would.

Amrik yawned. —Get real, Vinda.

—Okay, so he's not exactly a boyfriend. We just have this agreement, yeah? He's got this need. I need some cash. Sorted.

—Oooh my, sounds ideal. Do I hear wedding bells?

—Oh for God's sake. Why am I trying to justify myself to you of all people? You know I didn't just pick him up off the street.

—What then?

Vinda grit her teeth. —Damn it, Amrik. She paused. —You know what your problem is, don't you? She cleared her throat. —You hang out in all the divey places. How can you expect more than a twenty when you're prowling around King's Cross?

Amrik let out a long breath. —You're right. But where am *I* going to find a big-bucks lawyer?...Hey, he snapped his fingers, —Why don't you ask Derek whether he knows anyone?

—Amrik! Vinda sat up. — I can't ask Derek something like that.

—Why not? When you're putting the pliers to his nipples you can just ask him whether he has a friend—

—I *won't*.

—Fine. Don't help your friends. Be like that... *sadist*.

Vinda yawned. —Okay, okay, I'll see what I can do. God, Amrik, I'm trying to get out of this mess, but you just draw me deeper into it.

—Oh sure. Blame me if it makes you feel better.

Vinda laughed.

Amrik giggled, then inhaled sharply. —Shit, it's nearly half-twelve. I've got to get to Russell Square now before all the cute boys are taken.

—Go on then. And remember, if there are only old ones left, take the money first.

—Oh please, Vinda, what do you take me for?

She chuckled. —Nothing less than eighty quid.

When Vinda slunk into the kitchen to forage for leftovers, she found her uncle standing by the kettle swinging a tea bag over his mug. His eyes squinted over flaps of cheek. —I say, niece! Are you going to make tea now?

Vinda scowled. —No, Uncle Aloy, I'm just going to eat something.

—Ahh. Uncle Aloy's eyes widened for a moment. — *My* God, only now you are eating? Why so late? Where have you been? He giggled. —Must be with some bloke getting tickled under the covers, no? Maybe with some ahz-hole?

Vinda sneered. —No 'ahz-holes', I'm afraid, just some friends. She opened the fridge and took out some plastic containers. —Did you have supper, Uncle?

Uncle Aloy watched the steam spurting from the kettle. —Supper? No, no. My wife is punishing me.

—Punishing you? Vinda opened a tub of Dairylea spread and scooped fried aubergine onto her plate. — Why, what have you done this time?

—I? Nothing, *men*. Your Aunty, don't you know. She's mad.

Vinda watched her uncle stir sugar into his tea. —Hey, isn't that bad for you?

—Shhh. Uncle Aloy held the spoon in mid-air. —She'll hear you. It was just a little anyway.

Vinda sighed. —Do you want me to serve you some rice while I have everything out?

Uncle Aloy shook his head. —No, no. I don't want any. I have already eaten.

—But you just said that you haven't eaten supper.

—I know, I know. He took a sip from his mug. —I had some dried fish and rice just now.

—No wonder she's punishing you. You must have stunk up the whole place frying that fish. Vinda sniffed the air. —Yeah, I can still smell it—

—Quiet, *men*. You sound just like her. He shook his head. —You de Zoysa women are all the same.

—And just what is that supposed to mean?

Uncle Aloy chuckled. —Bad with the good, no? My wife had very nice thighs in those days. That's why I married her. He studied the rim of his cup. —Now she's filled out a bit.

—So? Vinda removed her plate from the microwave. —It's not as though you've much more to offer.

—I? Uncle Aloy's eyes travelled across Vinda's chest. —I can still please a young woman.

Vinda shrugged. —So you're sure you don't want anything for dinner then. Fine. She picked up her plate and walked out of the kitchen.

—Oy, Uncle Aloy called after her, —niece, aren't you going to make—?

Vinda was up the stairs and in her room before her uncle could finish his sentence. She plunged her fingers into the steaming heap of rice and pork, shovelling it into her eager mouth. All that whipping and shouting certainly drained one's energy, she mused. But she wasn't really complaining, after all, it was money, money that she badly needed. Her rent was due by the end of the week, and although it was to be paid to her aunt, she still felt obliged to be punctual about it. There was no question of ever handing a rent cheque to her uncle, though. He'd probably try to export another car to Sri Lanka part by part, she thought. Only two years ago he had gone to Heathrow and pleaded with a fellow passenger to empty out his suitcase.

—Come now, he had said, —don't worry, it's a simple operation. No one will know. The man's eyes had grown progressively wider. —What, *men?* Nothing to fear. Just put the tyre in and put your clothes in your hand-luggage. The man had shook his head. —You don't understand, Uncle Aloy had continued, —those bloody arseholes only took the four tyres, they forgot the spare. Do you see? The man had nodded. —Ahhh. Good. So now, how?

The man had walked away. Uncle Aloy had raised his arms in desperation, then shook his head from side to side. —Bloody useless buggers, he had muttered.

Vinda didn't know whether he finally got the tyre to Sri Lanka; all she knew was that the Benz was waiting somewhere in some godforsaken warehouse along with the Morris Minors and one 1987 model BMW. She snorted. Madman, she thought. In that moment she laughed off the countless unwanted caresses he showered on her with his leathery palm. She decided to forgive, or at least forget, the hand that appeared like city smog curling and peeling over her thigh whenever he gave her a lift into town. Now she refused all offers of a ride into central London – or anywhere else – unless it was crucial.

But Uncle Aloy found other ways of satisfying his need to touch young flesh. A surreptitious grazing of the buttocks as Vinda bent down to search the kitchen cupboards, or a casual stroke of her hip as she vacuumed the carpets in his bedroom. It was done in the simplest manner, without a single misplaced groan or giggle, but Vinda knew exactly what he was up to and occasionally ran the hoover over his bare toes in retribution. It wasn't serious enough to warrant a holocaust in the house, she decided, so she tolerated his advances, keeping her back to the wall if ever they were both inhabiting the same cramped space.

Later, as she crept up the stairs after visiting the kitchen for the last time that night, her aunty called out to her from the bedroom. —Is that you, Asma? Vinda stamped her foot on the first landing, flinching at the sound of that name. Asma. Some kind of cruel trick played on her by her father, lover of things Greek.

—Why did he have to name me after a chest condition? she had whined to her mother when she became better acquainted with her family's chronic health problems. —And where were you anyway? How could you let him do that to me? Her mother shook her head and stroked her daughter's hair, not having the heart to explain that Asma meant 'song' in ancient Greek before it ever became associated with a breathing disorder.

It was with revenge in her heart and a touch of irony that she seized on the garish nickname given to her by some spotty English boy during a brief fuck between classes. —You're hotter than a...a...a...He was pushing into her, clutching her sweating backside away from the teacher's desk. —A *vindaloo*.

—Vindaloo? she said, wrinkling her nose. —As in the curry?

—Yeah, he smiled, kissing her gently on the cheek and hugging her close. —You're my little spicy curry girl, my sexy Vindaloo.

She smiled weakly, and within a week let him go, spitting: — Next time you want a curry, order a bleeding takeaway.

But she had taken that name and made it her own. She was Vinda the invincible, Vinda the enflaming, Vinda the dominatrix. And yet her aunty persisted in calling her Asma, the name itself a wheeze in the throat.

—Asma? Why are you so late?

Vinda turned and stood in the bedroom doorway. —I know it's late, Aunty Agnes. How are you tonight?

—Oh, all right. She turned her head towards Vinda's darkened silhouette. —My legs are paining a little, but otherwise I'm fine.

Vinda walked in and flopped herself on the foot of the bed. —What's the family goss like these days?

—What? Aunty Agnes laughed. —Well, nothing much really.

—Any news from California?

—Kathy is having another baby.

—Really? But I thought she got divorced.

—She is.

—Does she have a new boyfriend?

—A boyfriend? Aunty Agnes scratched her elbow. — No, *men*. What boyfriends for her? She's decided she's a less-bian now.

Vinda stifled a giggle. —Oh . . . so, where does she live?

—In her apartment, I suppose. She sounded irritated. —She and her *friend* are going to bring up the baby. *Ayyo*, what that child will be like, God only knows.

—But who's the father?

Aunty Agnes shrugged. —She won't say. No one knows. She sighed. —What to do? She says she's happy. She searched her scalp with the tip of an index finger. — Just like her father, she is. I give this new one a year, like all the others.

—You mean there were other women? Vinda stared at her aunty.

—No, no. But there were so many others, *men*. One must have been the father.

Vinda nodded. She rolled onto her back to stare at the stucco ceiling. —Whatever happened to Uncle Nimal anyway? Is he still in California?

—Oh yes. He's a Hari Krishna now. A holy man. He told Kathy that no meat-eaters are allowed to enter his house.

—So, does Kathy see much of him then?

—Yes, very often. Anyway, this Nimal is mad. He has a new woman now, an Indian. A vegetarian I suppose. She giggled and her entire girth trembled beneath the duvet. —When he wants a nice steak he'll have to leave this one and find someone else.

—A Hari Krishna. Vinda chuckled. —And Kathy? Is she still Church of God?

Aunty Agnes pulled absently at a strand of black hair. —That one? I don't know. One day she's a Church of God, another day she's a Hari Krishna, another she's Muslim, and the next she's a devotee of Sai Baba. Now she's a bloody less-bian. What to do, child?

Vinda yawned. She heard the stairs creak, and quickly bent to kiss her aunt on the cheek.

—Oy, what are you two ladies doing in the bed? Uncle Aloy appeared in the doorway. —You-all are the same. Without a man you go mad.

—Just shut up, *men*. Aunty Agnes shifted her weight abruptly. —You have a bloody filthy mind.

He giggled. —Calm down, Agnes. Turning his eyes on Vinda he whispered. —Your aunty has a fiery temper, he approached the bed, murmuring, —and good thighs.

—What? Aunty Agnes sat up in bed. —Get out of here without talking your damn nonsense.

Vinda jumped from the bed. —Night all.

She slipped quickly from the room and up the stairs. As she opened her bedroom door she heard the distant warbling of her uncle, —Love bells are ringing for me and my cow.

In a rare breach of etiquette, Derek asked Vinda to meet him at a bar the following Thursday. —Wear something nice, he had said, and Vinda shrugged at the telephone. She brought her gear as usual, this time in a patent leather backpack.

When she walked into Village Soho, she stared at the walls, looking for Derek among crowds of immaculate young men. They talked easily with one another, shifting their eyes constantly to follow the movement of well-fitting 501s or a ribbed torso. She saw Derek standing by the bar, sipping from a Martini glass. He waved her over, pointing to his glass and crooking his head to the side. She nodded. As soon as she reached him, he pushed a fresh Martini towards her. —Thanks. Why the special meeting?

Derek kissed his teeth. —I'm fine, and how are you?

Vinda dismissed him with a flip of her hand. —I don't usually drink Martinis, but thank you. She sipped tentatively. —Glad to know you're fine, so am I.

—Do you want to go upstairs? It might be more comfortable for you . . . more women.

—Isn't it Dyke Night up there? Derek nodded. Vinda sneered. —Dying to check out the women even if they're not interested in you?

They made their way up the stairs. —Why not? Derek cupped the air with up-turned palms. —Some of them are very sexy.

Vinda snorted. —Well, I guess I can't argue with you there.

They carved out a space by the bar, and ordered another two drinks. Derek and Vinda scanned the room.

—What do you think of her? Derek pointed to a dark-haired woman in a fitted, blue T-shirt.

Vinda stared for a moment. —Not bad. Like the T-shirt.

Derek nodded. —She's got great hair, don't you think?

—Too long, Vinda wrinkled her nose, —but very healthy, I'll admit. Blue T-shirt caught Vinda through the corner of her eye. —Oh my God, Vinda grabbed Derek's wrist dramatically, —she's looking at me. She smiled quickly. —Actually, she's kind of cute, don't you think?

Derek ordered another drink. —Have you eaten yet? He played with the cuffs of his shirt.

—Not really. Vinda slit her eyes. —Why?

—Stop behaving like a caged animal, Vinda. He exhaled gruffly. —I'd like to go out to dinner with you. How about Soho Soho? It's on me.

Vinda frowned for a second, then sighed. —Okay. Why not?

As they left Brewer for Old Compton Street, Derek bent toward Vinda's ear. —I don't know how to tell you this, but your Blue T-shirt—

Vinda's eyes widened. —What about her?

—She pinched my bum.

Vinda stopped walking. —What? When?

—As we were leaving. Derek laughed. —What do you think of that?

—What an insult, Vinda chuckled. —I mean *you* and not me? She placed a hand on her chest. —I'm sure she was just too shy. You know, go for the lesser when you're intimidated.

—Believe what you will. Derek held the door open as Vinda walked through. —You can heal yourself with some decent food.

Vinda stepped inside. —I suppose, she stared grimly at the glittering crowd, —I suppose I haven't a choice.

Voices bounced incoherently against clay tiling and glass panes as Vinda inserted and withdrew the tines of her fork from a square of lasagne. She looked absently at Derek, watching his mouth move as he spoke. She didn't blink when he stopped talking, but continued to stare at a fleck of basil stuck in the cleft below his lip.

—Don't you hate it when that happens?

Vinda peered at the tiny shred of green. —Yeah, it's really embarrassing.

Derek scowled. —What? He shook his head and grunted, —You haven't been listening at all, have you?

—Sorry, I'm a little preoccupied.

—Still thinking of the woman in the tight T?

—Who? She looked at Derek's face as it reddened with irritation. —No. I was...I mean, do you mind telling me what this is all about? Why are we here? Aren't we supposed to—

Derek held up his palm. —Later, later. Right now I just feel like having a chat with you. He paused. —And if you must know, I haven't eaten since eleven-thirty this morning, so I thought... and anyway, why are you complaining so much? He glanced at Vinda's excavating fork. —What's wrong? Don't you like it?

Vinda immediately ceased poking her lasagne. —No, no. I was just thinking. She pushed a forkful into her mouth. —Actually, it's very good. Not a bad place really.

Derek chewed idly on a piece of olive bread. —What did you study, Vinda? In college, I mean.

—Why do you want to know?

Derek let out a heavy breath. —Just *tell* me.

Vinda drew her lips into a tense pout. —English Literature. She smiled tightly. —I did it for the enjoyment. But it ended up being a bit disappointing, too much theory, not enough literature. What do I know about 'terror' and the 'colonial encounter'? Her mouth drooped elaborately. —I don't read very much anymore. Just the odd magazine. She returned to her food. —Do you enjoy being a lawyer?

Derek grinned. —Of course. I like dealing in semantic minutiae. And the money is good. He looked at Vinda. — It allows me a few luxuries.

Vinda raised a brow. —Good thing there are a few dullards like myself around to keep you amused for a small price.

Derek coloured. —I shouldn't describe you as a dullard. If you were, why should I want to meet you so frequently? Do you think I'm a fool?

Vinda shifted in her chair. —I suppose I should be flattered to be counted amongst your luxuries. She glanced at the table next to theirs where two middle-aged, wine-faced men sat drinking with a young woman.

—Let's go to the O Bar, the larger one said to his colleague.

—The O Bar, piped an American voice. She was blond, and her lips slid along the top and bottom of the 'O' until they met, sending it up like a soap bubble. —That's a great idea. The large man winked at his friend.

Vinda turned away. —Where to next?

Derek placed a hand on Vinda's. —The usual. I have some good grass at the studio as well.

—Sounds good. She backed her chair away from the table and stood up. —Let's go.

As they stepped out onto the street, Derek cleared his throat. —I hope you don't mind walking a little.

—Didn't you bring the car?

—I left it by the flat, actually.

Vinda rubbed her hands together. —No worries. I need some movement right now. They headed down Frith

Street towards Soho Square. She turned to Derek. —
Don't you get tired of having two places to live in?

—Don't you?

—What do you mean? What – my life? She blinked. —
What do you know about my life? She kneaded her palm
with a thumb. —Anyway, everyone has two lives. It
makes things interesting, at least.

—Does it?

—It pays.

Derek placed a conspiratorial hand against his mouth.

—And are you claiming?

Vinda slowed her pace. —What do you care?

He shrugged. —I don't really.

She glanced at the brittle steps of St George's. —I
know you make quite a bit of money, she peered at its
grime-stained columns, —but how can you afford two
flats?

Derek winked. —I share it.

—I see. Vinda nodded. —So you all have your little bit
on the side.

—Not all. I share with one other guy. It makes things
much cheaper.

—I can imagine. She dug her hands into her pockets.
—By the way, she said watching the pavement slide by
beneath her, —do you know anyone who's into boys—
men boys, I mean?

—What? Why?

—I've got a friend... Vinda watched two women
kissing by the traffic light. One was in a leather jacket
and jeans, the other wore a long, flared coat.

—Interested? Derek prodded Vinda.

Vinda rolled her eyes. —Well? Do you?

—What? Know anyone who's into boys? Vinda
nodded. —Sure. Do you want me to arrange something?

They were approaching Derek's flat.

—Maybe. I'll let you know.

When they were inside, Vinda took her bag and headed for the bathroom. Derek caught her arm. —Hey, wait. Vinda backed away. He quickly removed his hand. —I just . . . I thought we could have that joint first.

Vinda scratched the back of her neck. —Derek. Look, how am I supposed to work if I'm stoned?

—Don't worry about it. I don't know if I want that tonight.

Vinda's eyes widened. —Why didn't you say that in the first place? Look at how much time you've wasted. Damn it, you know I can't afford to just hang out with you.

—Why not? What have you paid for so far?

—That's not the point. Vinda's hands were clenched against her hips. —This is supposed to be a professional exchange. Why are you complicating it this way?

—What complications have I created? Derek rubbed his chin. —You'll get your money, don't worry. Why don't you just enjoy the break?

Vinda stared at Derek. —All right, all right. She looked at his chin. —It's still there.

—What is?

—The basil, it's been there all night.

Derek dug a finger into his chin. —*Now* you tell me. His face darkened. —You know, sometimes you can be a right — He pursed and unpursed his lips, struggling to keep in his breath, then let it out in a huff —bitch.

Vinda threw her bag on the ground. —So where's this joint, anyway?

They passed it back and forth wordlessly. Vinda felt her knees go lax, and her shoulders droop. It wasn't such a bad idea, after all. What would Amrik say to this? Here she was, having had free Martinis, dinner and now a joint—*and* she was getting paid for it. —Too good, she said out loud, —too good.

Derek looked at the smirk on Vinda's face. —Good stuff, isn't it?

She gave Derek a wobbly smile. —Mmm . . . yeah. She began to laugh and Derek laughed with her. They were lying on the floor, knees up and swaying from side to side. —I was expecting my lips to start itching. She pulled at her lips. —They often do, some allergic reaction.

Derek giggled. —I've never heard of that before.

Vinda rolled her eyes towards Derek. —Never? But I know loads of people who've had a similar reaction. She paused for a moment. —Okay, maybe not loads. But I'm sure there was at least one other person . . .

—Vindaloo, Derek crooned, —Vindaloo, who are you? Vinda snorted. Derek turned over and placed his mouth against Vinda's ear. —What's your last name Vinda?

—Loo! She cried before a wave of high-pitched screeching fell from her lips.

—Shhh, shhh. Derek clasped a hand over Vinda's open mouth. She bit him. —Ow. He inhaled sharply. —Mmmm. That was . . . nmmmm. Please, do it again? Vinda frowned. She ground her teeth into the flesh of his hand until his mouth flew open in silent pain. He let out shivering moans, then twisted his hand hard against her teeth, feeling them dig into his skin.

Vinda jerked her face to the side. —Oi! she gasped, —get . . . get your . . . h-hand . . . off.

Derek didn't move. He stared at her with red-rimmed eyes, swallowing. —I'm getting pasty. I need some water. He removed his hand and got up.

Vinda remained still, breathing heavily. It didn't seem real. What was he playing at? Had he just tried to choke her? She felt thirsty. —Water, she whispered. Derek handed her a glass of water. She frowned. —You're back? How long have you been standing there? She reached out for the glass and drank. Eyes open, she saw waves of water rolling towards her. She heard it go down with loud gulps. Derek's face loomed like a jellyfish through the bottom of the glass. She closed her eyes and kept drinking. When she opened her eyes again Derek was lying by her side on the carpet. —You have a very low ceiling. Vinda blinked at the white space floating above her.

—It's not low. It's high. It's a high ceiling. Derek lifted his arm and pointed upward. —It's high, see?

Vinda saw Derek balancing the ceiling on the tip of his index finger. She reached up with her arm and felt nothing. —There's nothing there. She let her arm drop. —Is this real?

Derek turned over and put his arm around Vinda's waist. —Everything is real.

Vinda smiled and sighed. —de Zoysa, she said finally.

—What's that? Derek was breathing into her ear.

—My last name. Vinda had the vague sensation of a hand on her bare stomach, and felt her muscles unnumb beneath it. Closing her eyes, she tried to imagine the path of the hand. It seemed to be sliding under her panties and between her breasts at the same time. She could feel the blood collecting just under her skin.

Vinda opened an eye and saw Derek's neck straining above her. With a jerk of her shoulders she tried to topple him, but he was too heavy. Her lips parted with the effort, letting loose a gush of air. —What are you doing? she heard herself say. Her voice hit the ceiling and split into waves. —Get off, you bastard. An echo. Her eyes rolled back as he moved deeper into her, slamming the base of her spine against the rug.

—Nmmmm . . . nmmmm . . . nmmmm, he whimpered. She felt something dribbling into her ear. —*Get off me*. —Nmmmm. . . nmmmm . . . nmmmm—

Her face was wet, though she knew she was not crying. Vinda's limbs refused to move. She lay pinned beneath Derek, shouting, as he wept fat tears onto her cheeks.

Vinda woke up with her patent leather bag by the foot of the bed. She was alone, lying in a room she could not recall entering. She sifted through the pile of clothes beside her, snatching up her underpants quickly. Buttoning up her blouse, she walked from room to room looking for Derek. He was gone. She returned to the bedroom to get her bag. As she picked it up, she noticed a roll of paper protruding from one of the pockets. She pulled it out, unravelling it as she did so. It was an envelope. —As promised, it said. In it was exactly eighty-five pounds. Vinda bit her lip, counting the notes carefully. —Son of a bitch, she spat, and folded them into her wallet.

THERAPY
Sharon Jennings

5.01

Fifty-nine minutes until this torture would end. The mounting tension at the back of her neck was on course to becoming a full-blown migraine and would soon be impossible to ignore. Anita Moss tugged at the denim skirt that fitted snugly against her plump thighs, knowing it would never reach her knees no matter how hard she pulled. She then wriggled and shifted her bottom on the director-style chair until she reached something akin to comfortable. She forced herself to stop thinking about later, she couldn't decide anyway, and aimed a disinterested gaze towards Clare Denton who sat opposite, clutching both arms of her chair.

Anita had just finished her Counselling Psychology degree when she heard about the groundbreaking Kalou Women's Mental Health Association in West Bridge. The newly opened centre had already made a name for itself in helping mentally distressed women from all backgrounds and lifestyles free of charge. That was eight years ago and Anita, with her then shoulder-length locks which she wore adorned with colourful headwraps, loved the idea of stamping out the kind of racism or homophobia that these women faced in trying to seek help. She wanted so badly to help them. Abused women, that was her calling.

It meant moving away from her family and friends and striking out on her own. That too was enticing, Anita needed to get away. Her course at university had been great; she liked learning about people and what makes them do the things they do. But she had remained at home during her studies. At the age of twenty-two she had been ready to leave it all behind. The centre had been where she felt destined to be.

Kalou was purpose-built and modern, the bare wood floors, plush furniture and pale blues and lavenders in the colour scheme were meant to induce a sense of neutral serenity. It was a friendly centre with a devoted staff group and Anita had loved her job. She was one of the more popular counsellors and her clients often spoke about her to their friends. 'She's black, you know, and she's got long locks . . . she dresses a little like a hippie but that's cool' . . . 'She's not that old, about twenty-five or thirty, I guess, but she's good and she doesn't talk your business to anybody else' . . . were her key attributes along with the kindness and understanding she showed.

But today, she had really struggled: through the 9.30 domestic violence who was going back anyway; the 11.00 rape who had taken tablets, but not enough to kill herself; the 1.30 pregnant again but didn't want to be; and the 3.00 depression because she came out at work and now no one will talk to her. She didn't know how she had managed to get to 5.03, with Clare Denton in full flow.

Anita nodded and smiled in the right places, trying not

to show resentment to Clare. Clare never failed to arrive looking immaculate even though her appointment was at the end of her working day. Anita fantasised that Clare would rush home to shower and apply fresh make-up and clothing just to make her feel shabby. And it never failed.

Today she was dressed in a pale pink trouser suit and matching turban-style headwrap, in comparison to Anita's short-sleeved T-shirt and tacky denim skirt that had always been too tight for her ample hips and thighs. At least she had worn her favourite shoes.

In contrast with her measured fashion sense, Clare spoke rapidly, incoherently, and avoided any eye contact with Anita.

...She had had a terrible week. It started when she arrived an hour and a half late on Monday...

Her speech was monotonal, filling the small windowless room with her droning.

...It was because of the traffic...but her manager is a cow and didn't believe her...

Her gaze shifted around the room, never lingering on any item for too long. On she went, every so often eyeing the one poster that graced the otherwise bare lavender wall.

...Anyway, her workmates were jealous of her...

Rigid no more, her body began twisting and agitating in the chair; her legs crossing, uncrossing in time with her words.

...They went off her ever since she was promoted...

Her right foot had started keeping time with her speech. Jiggling wildly until it knocked against the small table holding a vase with two pink hyacinths and a box of Kleenex.

...Even her boyfriend Earl was taking the piss...

Now her face took up the pace, wincing and puckering as she tried to force the words out.

. . . Oh yeah, did she say she went out with her girlfriends and got too drunk?

Her pitch was high, the drone replaced with a whine.

. . . It was hard to stay slim but she was lucky that food didn't stick to her . . .

5.08!

. . . Oh, had the room been painted?

5.10

. . . There was a robbery at her local supermarket last week but she only heard about it . . .

Anita took a deep breath and tried not to sound too abrupt. With what she hoped was a level but firm tone, she broke in, 'Is this what you've come to talk about today, Clare?'

Clare froze for a second, as if she had been slapped and then dissolved into tears. When her hiccuping had subsided she dabbed gently at her swollen eyes with a sodden tissue and sat looking at Anita as if for permission to start again. This was the usual occurrence.

Clare just needed time to settle in before telling her story which she told at the same frantic pace as before, trying to get the nasty words out as fast as she could. Clare's story was one that Anita was familiar with, one she didn't want to hear at all today.

Clare had been abused by her uncle, when she was too young to understand anything about it except her own fear whenever she went to visit him. Normally, Anita's heart went out to Clare, she really did care about her, but today she found it hard to stay tuned in.

'I've been writing in my diary like you told me but it doesn't help. He phoned and I know you said I don't have to talk to him but I did. He told me he was going to be at my parents' at Christmas and looked forward to seeing me. Nobody knows about him.'

Anita tried to keep her neutral gaze on Clare and not look at the clock (it was only 5.15). Her head was getting worse, pounding like it was trying to match the speed and rhythm of Clare's gush. One more session after this and, and then what... she hadn't decided.

'I don't know if I should tell anyone in my family, you see. It was suchalongtimeagobutthere'smyniece-whois...'

Anita took a tissue and wiped invisible sweat from her brow.

'... aboutthesameageasIwaswhenhestartedyouknowand IthinkIshouldwarnmysister...'

Anita coughed lightly hoping that would keep down the nausea that was rising in her throat.

'... maybedoyouthinkhemighthavedonethesamething to...'

...Anita made a clack-clack, clack-clack sound as she walked down the street in her church shoes. Mammie had let her wear the shiny black ones with the double strap and the pink bow that used to belong to her cousin. Looking down at the shoes, her new shoes, the white-white ankle socks that Mammie washed by hand, and her shiny brown legs, she smiled for the first time that week. As she walked to Sunday School she smoothed down the front of her crisply starched, faded blue dress and reached behind her to feel if the big faded blue bow was still tied. Satisfied that it was, she allowed herself another smile; everything was right.

She felt happy that morning, clack-clacking down the street, glad to get away from Mammie and Daddy who were just starting to fight. They probably didn't know that she had left the house. But, after all, she was a big girl of nine and didn't need anyone to walk with her. She approached Mr Lenno's house and saw that the front door was open. His house wasn't as nice as her house but it had a big wooden swing on the porch and sometimes on the way home from school, he would let her swing. The metal chain was rusty and creaked when she sat on the swing. Mr Lenno said he needed to oil it and would she like to watch him when he did.

Mr Lenno told her funny stories about troublesome children and the bad things that could happen to them. When he finished, he would always put his hand inside his big flappy trouser pocket and shake it. It would be full of coins and jingle like Christmas bells. She loved this part and felt excited as he slipped a few coins into her expectant hand and putting his finger to his lips he would say, 'Shhh.' This was their little secret.

Mr Lenno was standing at the front door, still in his bathrobe. You not going to church this morning, sir? You not feeling too well? She stepped carefully up the walkway so that he too could hear the clack-clack, clack-clack of her shiny new shoes. Do you like my shoes? Listen to this. Clack-clack, clack-clack. Mr Lenno opened the front door to let her in. She eyed the swing, now motionless as she entered.

The living room was dark and smelled like dust and something that Daddy drank on Saturday nights. Mr Lenno was a nice man and she liked him very much. He had made her laugh and let her swing on his squeaky swing whenever she wanted. She wanted to now but Mr Lenno said no, not today. He wanted her to stay inside today. She remembered that Mammie said to respect and obey grown-up people.

*

Anita's face was burning hot as she tried to keep her focus on Clare.

'. . . OhIstillhavedreamswheresomeoneischasingme downadarkstreetandIkeep running but I can't seem to get away, no matter how fast I go, he is still behind me. I never see the face of the person but I know it's a man and I know it's him.'

She got a beating that afternoon for coming home an hour late from the Sunday School that she never attended. Daddy, still in his vest, slapped the leather belt hard on her shiny brown legs while she stared down at her new shoes with the double strap and pink bow. As the tears trickled down her face for the second time that day, she was still glad that she hadn't got her blue dress dirty; the bow was still tied.

Clare had stopped talking and sat utterly still. Tears stood up boldly in her eyes, ready to overflow down her face. She looked like a sad, lonely little girl and Anita suddenly had the urge to take her in her arms and hold her for the rest of the session. Despite the throbbing dizziness, she fought to find the right words.

'Clare, please go on. I know it's hard, it's painful, but it will help you to talk about it, not keep it bottled up inside. It was not your fault. You must remember that. It was never your fault. You were just a child. Clare. Please go on.'

She never told Mammie and Daddy because Mr Lenno said she mustn't be troublesome or he'd come late at night and kill her in her bed if she did. She hid her blood-sticky knickers in the secret gap she had found between the floorboard and the wall behind her wardrobe.

Anita's headache was now at full pitch and she knew she would not be able to endure this much longer.

'Please go on, Clare.'

At 6.00 Anita accompanied Clare to the door. She was still dabbing at her eyes with a fresh tissue. It had been a heavy session but Clare managed a smile, despite her swollen eyes. 'I don't know how this is helping, Anita, but I do feel better. Thank you.'

Anita too managed a smile, though somewhat strained. 'See ya next week, Clare. Take care.'

Anita barely made it to the toilet in time. Otherwise she would have puked all over the lavender carpet and pale green walls. Emerging from the end stall, the mini-spotlight reflecting off the white tiles and large mirror was too much and she had to leave the room before she fainted.

She staggered back to her desk and was conscious that all the other staff had gone except Barbara, the cleaner, who was probably at the other end of the building having a cup of tea, or something stronger, if the rumours were true. Fumbling through her bag she found her painkillers and downed three without the aid of water. The acrid aftertaste compelled her to the staff kitchen to make a coffee and overload it with four sugars.

Loping back to her desk, mug clasped between her palms, she glanced at the clock. Her next appointment would be in twenty minutes and she still had to write up her session with Clare, dredging up the debris of that last hour to make sure she was accountable for her work. She always hated this part and often put it off until she was reminded by her manager that her files were not up to date. Anita sat at her desk and sipped her coffee.

She had so much to think about right now, but she knew

she was not in a fit state to make any decisions. The coffee was finished but she couldn't face making another one. Fighting back the tears she felt weary; all she wanted was to lay her hot achy head onto the cool surface of her uncluttered desk and sleep for ever. It was getting worse. The empty swing creaking in the wind, Mr Lenno shaking his pocket for change, the bloody knickers. Blood. The images were coming all the time now; breaking through the barriers she had worked so hard to build up over the years. She couldn't make him go away. Couldn't make them go away. The jangle of the phone slapped her upright.

'Hello, Kalou Women's Mental Health, how can I help you?' She sounded professional, alert and interested. She took up her favourite pen with the black and silver yin/yang design and sat poised to take a message.

'Hi, girl. Is that you? Why you there so late?' Deborah sounded friendly again.

'Hi, Deb. Just got one more session and I'm off. How are you?' She asked this cautiously and steeled herself for whatever answer Deb would give. Last night had been excruciating and the best friends had not parted on good terms.

'Oh, okay. But still thinking about last night. Look, uh, you want to stop by on your way home?'

Anita might have plans. She didn't know if she could tonight.

'No, sorry, Deb. I've, uh, I might have something on. Sorry.' This last 'sorry' faded and was barely audible.

'Oh, I see. You're still pissed off about last night, is that it?'

'No, no, that's not it. Only I . . .'

'Look, I care about you and someone has to tell you the truth.'

'Deborah, I don't want to start this up again. Okay?

You don't like what I do and that's that. I don't want to talk about it any more, if you don't mind.'

'Don't mind! No, I don't mind. I don't mind anything. I don't mind that my best friend is slogging her guts out for pennies, being used to make our women grateful and believe they're happy. And you know that's true so don't deny it.'

Anita had met Deborah three years ago at a community meeting held at Kalou. Deborah was 'political', which meant she was against anything she felt enslaved black people and stopped them getting angry and taking to the streets. She thought counselling did just this. But for some reason she and Anita had struck up a sincere friendship and Anita liked Deborah's quick wit and sometimes stinging tongue. That is until she turned it on Anita. She made her feel ashamed to do the work she did. Ashamed and wrong.

There were times when Anita was able to come back at Deborah if not with a winning argument then at least with something rational. But tonight, close to tears, her stomach churning, her mind like mush, she didn't have the strength to battle with Deborah. She just wanted to hang up, but couldn't.

'Deborah, look, you don't know what you're talking about. It's not like that. But anyway...'

'No, I tell you what I don't know. I don't know what you think you're doing, messing around in people's shit. What gives you the right, surely not your degree or whatever it is you have? Make women talk so they can come to terms with things, that's what you do, isn't it? How is that supposed to help? Nita, they should be jumping up and down raging about it.'

Tonight, Anita couldn't say anything in her own defence.

'You know what I'd do if I was you? I'd stop all the talk, talk, talk, and *do* something. Take some action!'

'Deborah!' Anita suddenly choked with tears. 'I have to go now. I can't talk. I have to write up... and then... I'm not feeling well. Look I'm sorry...'

Deborah could be so insensitive. 'You're supposed to be so intelligent but you just don't get it. You know what they need? They need a good dose of revenge. Get back at the bastards. That's what I'd tell them.'

'Deb, you can't... Please. I'm trying to help them but I can't tell them to... I can't do that.'

'Why not? Anyway I can't talk sense into you. You're trying to be the Black Mother Teresa, aren't you? Well, good luck.'

Click, the dial tone. Deborah had gone.

The tears started to flow and Anita couldn't stop them. She sat sobbing and shaking, the phone receiver still clutched in her left hand, her favourite pen still poised in her right. Maybe talking didn't help. What if Deborah was right? Mother Teresa might have been a saint, but Anita didn't think that her clients loved her at all. They came, oh yes they came, but they dreaded coming. She was the woman who would drag them back through the barbed wire of their worst memories and they would have a damn sight more nightmares and cry a lot more tears before she was finished with them.

6.20

Through her tears she saw the clock. She would not be able to cope with Milly Kenyatta tonight. She always arrived late and wanted to still get her full hour. She was rude and never apologised. She treated Anita with disdain, often looked like she wanted to spit on her. Milly had been raped then beaten by her stepfather when she was five and couldn't stop finding abusive men just like him to fall in love with. Anita would not be able to listen to Milly tonight.

Shaking her head hard, she had no time for tears. She had a job to do: for Clare Denton; for Diane Manners who at the age of forty still had to sleep with the light on; for Ayodele Akappo whose twelve-year-old daughter had reported to the police she had been molested by her mother's fiancé; and all the others who came to see her who needed a mental refuge and vindication.

'Stop it damn it. I won't cry.' She tried her old childhood trick of squeezing her eyes hard shut and counting to twenty. And it worked, for when she opened her eyes the tears were gone. However, they were replaced with an urge to laugh. Anita felt the giggle rising up from her belly. 'Oh shit. And they say the first sign of madness is talking to yourself.' She let out a raucous howl.

'And the second sign is laughing about it.'

Anita found Barbara in the kitchen reading the paper while she waited for the kettle to boil. Of course, luv, Barbara would be happy to give a message to Milly and yes she would remember to apologise and say that Anita would phone her tomorrow, or maybe the day after. She was sorry that Anita was feeling so unwell, yes she looked pale, she meant pale for her kind of people that is.

Driving down Harlton Road, Anita grimaced, not liking the way her engine sounded. It must be time for a service, she thought, making a mental note that she would no doubt forget. Diane Manners had spoken with fondness of the years she had spent at Flat 2 in the care of her grandparents, Lillian and Wilton.

Anita parked opposite the block of mansion flats and sat for a moment, surveying the deserted street before getting out of the car. She suddenly felt a chill and remembered she'd left her cardigan at work, in the rush to get out. When Diane was thirteen Lillian had died, leaving her alone with Wilton. They continued to live in Flat 2 until Diane could take no more and ran away when she was sixteen and pregnant.

Anita could see from the plaque on the entrance door that Flat 2 was on the ground floor.

Half an hour later, as she gingerly stepped over the body of Wilton Manners, Anita was surprised that she didn't feel sick any more. She had to be careful to avoid the pool of blood that was spreading around his head. She said a silent 'sorry' for the mess she was leaving behind for someone (probably a woman) to clean up.

The little revolver fit neatly back into her handbag and had proven more reliable at close range than at longer distances. As she closed the door of the flat and made her way to her car, she made a mental note to cross Mr Wilton Manners off her list and to one day tell Deborah she was right. One day.

Anita Moss loved the clack-clack, clack-clack as she walked down the street to her car. She looked down at her shiny black shoes and smiled.

THREE FLAVOURS ON A PLATE

Saradha Soobrayen

For Hugh

'Trust me. You'll like this. You won't want to eat anything else,' he said, slapping a pork chop on my plate. It had been baked in the oven covered with thick condensed mushroom soup, ensuring the moisture of the chop while retaining the crispness of the rind. It was served with dumplings, crispy potatoes and a steamed pudding for dessert.

I often visited his table after skipping breakfast and missing lectures. It was my first year of university and he was my first taste of something new. I was also courted with liver, onions and bacon served in a gravy of their own juices. It was the simplicity of three flavours on a plate that worked for me; my fork never lazy, moving from one flavour to another, varying the sequence each time.

I admired his commitment to convention and the heaviness of his loving left me well-fed for days. I couldn't cook. But I loved to interfere. That was the seed of the trouble between us. I was fast and loose with spices and herbs, desperate to be a part of the making of a dish.

Halfway through the autumn term he became a vegetarian. Said he'd been thinking about it for some time and yet he couldn't say if it was the plight of the calves and lambs in cargo or the foot and mouth crisis or BSE which had finally turned him round.

'Trust me. You'll like this. You won't want to eat meat ever again.'

He tried to drown my pleas for gravy with a wave of Mexican dishes, huge ripe tomatoes, soya mince, spices and guacamole. At first I was swayed by his new-found regime and he allowed me to chop the vegetables and stir the great vat of sauce. He believed in the versatility of soya and tomatoes and used the same basic dish to fill tacos, tortillas, lasagnes and spaghetti Bolognese.

I agreed to vegetarianism in principle but my imagination let me down. Next to him I would lie, moist, dreaming fry-ups, craving bacon and wake in the morning aching for the grizzle of summer barbecues. One of my earliest memories is of a chicken drumstick: I must have been three when I snapped the bone and sucked out the juicy marrow. Summer just wouldn't be the same without a barbecue.

I felt ignored and begged for a return to the pork chop suppers or even a fish dish. He couldn't be persuaded and continued to mould loose soya protein into burgers with his bare hands.

His kitchen was no longer safe. It became a war zone, with discontentment bubbling in the air. Eventually I was banned. I had contaminated a whole pan of soya mince with chilli sauce.

'You can't taste anything. It needed spice, it needed heat,' was my defence.

We began to have separate meals and separate lives but we did try to reconcile our differences and at least eat together once again. We went to a vegetarian restaurant with reasonable prices and we started off with reasonable manners and continued with reasonable conversation. But the divisions were deep; there was no conferring over menu choices. He was determined not to be swayed by my suggestions.

I believed in tactical ordering for the table, ensuring the best range of flavours and the possibility of endless combinations. He just pointed: 'My plate, your plate.'

Life without him became life without crockery. I had lapsed into squalor. The odd cup left in the sink became part of a stacked construction threatening to topple. I had no idea what to do or even how to begin to recreate the dishes that I needed. My kitchen was littered with burnt steaks and other failed attempts; it became obvious I had to look elsewhere for gratification. I needed a quick and easy fix, where I could get what I wanted, when I wanted, and not have to worry about washing up.

When I'd started university I had chosen to live in the notorious fast-food district, miles from any shops but well within the five-mile free delivery radius of most restaurants in town. Instead of asking neighbours about the quality of the streets, I'd made my decision by surveying menus in steamy takeaway windows.

I now began to leave my flat every night and return with wrapped paper parcels.

Shish kebabs, doner kebabs, chicken kebabs, mixed kebabs with onions and sauce, forget the salad, shredded lettuce, and sliced tomatoes. It was easy. It was shameless but it was juicy and for a few hours it silenced the nagging hunger in my stomach.

I ate more and more and I could feel my stomach

growing, never satisfied. I couldn't stop the endless takeaways; the chips, the battered fish. I felt cheap. But still I couldn't give it up – until a vicious bout of food poisoning landed me in hospital.

Stomach ache, vomiting, cramps. I couldn't believe I was at the mercy of a deli sandwich.

Pale-faced and grey-eyed, the thought of eating was torture to my senses. I saw everything I ate twice; on my plate and then in my sick bowl.

The hospital staff took pity on me and the night nurse in particular tried to settle my wrestling stomach with talk of wholefoods: lentils, barley, oatmeal; all the goodness of a vegan diet.

I became weak and my throat ached for mercy. I couldn't even keep water down. When the Christmas turkey slice platter was served with four brussels sprouts, a lonely steamed potato and no gravy, I wanted to be pronounced Nil by Mouth.

The night nurse encouraged me to eat the hospital slush. It was the only way I would heal. She tried to comfort me and told me I would feel worse before I got better. When she told me that I would be discharged the next day I panicked. I'd never felt so bad – my stomach was on fire and my lower back felt like it had been kicked. Even my joints were swollen. I wasn't sure if I could get up, but the bed was needed. She explained that once patients had been seen and treated they were discharged early and expected to recover in their own homes. I would be given my marching orders in the morning with repeat prescriptions for pink and white pills.

'Let me feed you what's good for you,' she said, holding my left wrist to check my pulse. Her words eased my nausea more effectively than any medication.

I was weak with hunger but my spirit was thirsty for adventure. I was being offered the chance to try other flavours, so again I renounced the flesh I so enjoyed and discharged myself into her house. She was devoted to salads, healing foods, raw foods: anything with vitamins still intact. It was a welcome relief to my grease-ridden stomach. I floated and flourished under the holistic attention. She cared for my insides and outsides. She knew what was in food and how best to eat it; chewing slowly and savouring the flavour and not just bolting it down.

It was spring and we slept light and ate light. We never had any puddings. She told me I was all the dessert she wanted. Every so often I would lie next to her and dream of my childhood birthdays: shop-bought Victoria sponges, the lace pattern of the icing sugar and the swirls of fresh cream.

She spoke about the evils of dairy produce, how it was mucus producing and how our bodies were constantly craving nutrients. She told me this was the reason I was always hungry; that my diet of junk food had left me desperate for the goodness which was missing from my life. I accepted her explanation, and let her lead me to a disease-free existence, cleansed of all pesticides and genetically modified products.

She told me not to worry about the future and that I was converting beautifully. I felt like an explorer discovering exotic fruit and vegetables. I knew in order to conquer her I would have to embrace veganism wholeheartedly.

One Sunday she served me breakfast in her garden. Miniature pancakes made with soya milk, cooked in dairy-free fat. Not the same as butter wafting in the air, but it did the trick. It got me out of bed, guided by my nose, and I could see she had really tried to be indulgent.

She dished up non-dairy ice cream, which was surprisingly delightful. I hadn't had ice cream for ages. I felt she brought out the child in me but it didn't make me want to stay and play. Veganism requires commitment and I lapsed. I began to eat around, finding excuses to drop in on friends, more interested in the contents of their fridges than their conversations.

I had a stash of vital ingredients – whole-grain mustard, chunky slices of white bleached bread – all to make sandwiches on the sly. Salami slices had to be smuggled into her house in my socks. One morning she got back early from her late shift at the hospital and found the bed empty. Usually she would wake me up with a tray laden with fresh apricots, sliced bananas and overripe kiwis. She knew I loved eating at least three distinct flavours at the same time.

The truckers' café was only five minutes' walk away. She used to walk past it coming back from her shift and had made the mistake of describing it to me. I told her not to walk that way if it disturbed her.

'It's a quicker way home to you,' she would say. 'All that carnage and untold damage to arteries, why do people do it?' she would ask, disgusted.

I knew why people did it and why they shouldn't. For weeks I had been sneaking out for bacon, runny eggs, sausages, beans, fried bread, fried mushrooms and black pudding. I went there early, giving myself enough time to eat, get back, wash and jump into bed ready for the mountain of fruit and whatever else she was willing to serve me. When she discovered I wasn't at the house she searched the streets until she found me. She stood outside the café, watching me wipe dripping bacon fat off my chin. I'll never forget the look on her face.

*

It was coming to the end of the summer term and I was left to my own devices once again. Cereal became my instant meal, dumped straight into half-full milk cartons. I just never got round to buying bowls. I spent a lot of time dreaming up food combinations that wouldn't hurt me, like galia melon slices the colour of peaches, draped with pink ribbons of smoked salmon, served with a spoonful of rhubarb purée.

I did wonder about going to see my mum. I had no idea what we would talk about. I hadn't spoken to her all year. Things had never been the same since she stopped cooking.

It happened gradually: she started serving the same meal over and over again. She had even stopped making my school sandwiches and began eating pickled onions with everything. She kept the catering-size jar on a side table near her armchair where she sat for hours staring at the television.

I didn't go home after the term ended. I knew what would have been waiting for me: orange-stained boil-in-the-bag kippers, served with grey mash and pickled onions.

Mum had lost the will to cook and Dad tried his best. He did huge Sunday roasts. He would start marinating the day before, warming whole cloves and slightly crushed cinnamon sticks in a pan and then he would mix some port with honey and let it all slide over a leg of lamb.

Dad liked to slow cook it to tenderness and then let it relax to release all its juices. I would feed on the smell even before it got to the table. Mum made sure she had her pickles. It didn't matter how hungry I was, Dad made me wait and the lamb was better for it. Dad and me couldn't help but munch and murmur harmonious contentment. His roasts would leave me paralysed for hours.

'You can't even get a decent cup of tea out of your mother,' was the last thing he said to me before he went to join the recently divorced baker's wife for a life of pastry.

Mum wouldn't touch meat after Dad left, let alone eat it. Fish in plastic was fine: coley in creamy sauce, cod in parsley. I never knew who to blame.

The most useful thing Mum ever said to me was, 'Make sure you find a place to live that's near a major supermarket.' I should have listened. I had always rejected her advice far too quickly, afraid that to accept would deny my own superior knowledge; but Mum was right when she said that the major supermarkets had everything you could possibly need in life. I liked going round in their revolving doors and there was something almost regal about them. They were like the new places of worship, the new places to congregate, and they made promises to anyone who would listen.

That summer I got a job on the deli counter: olives, hummus and, of course, cooked meats. Something inside me wanted to believe that they could deliver. I wanted to believe that a mug of real hot chocolate, dark in depth, delicately light in froth, was all I needed to keep me warm at night. I wanted to believe all that they said, like scrambled eggs made from their hand-picked range would create soft, peppered clouds of heaven on my plate and thickly buttered toast made with store-baked bread was the only way to start a working day. Most of all I wanted to believe that freshly-juiced Florida oranges, full of tingling bits, were as good as a morning kiss.

A DARKER SHADE OF BROWN

Nicola Sinclair

'Can I help you?'

On her doorstep stood a stately black man huddled beneath an oversized coat, his hands encased in heavy leather gloves. Circulatory problems, she thought. She never felt the cold. He looked up from his notebook to find a beautiful, honey-skinned black woman dressed in a thin white blouse and black skirt; her feet were bare and strangely pink.

'Yes, I'm looking for Miss, er,' he looked back at his notebook, momentarily distracted from his business, 'McEwan.'

She watched the silvery plumes of breath stream from his mouth as he talked; there was obviously some warmth to him.

'Aha, that's me.' She tucked a stray lock of her shoulder-length wavy brown hair behind her ear.

'Miss McEwan. I . . .'

'Please, call me Rhoda, it unnerves me when I'm referred to as Miss,' she interrupted.

'Oh, okay. Rhoda.' He stopped and thought. 'I don't

think I've ever met a Rhoda.'

'No, not many people have. I've never met another.'

'Unusual.'

'My mother was a big fan of American sitcoms. The love of her life has become the bane of mine.'

Rhoda stood in the doorway watching this man. He rubbed his gloved hand over his shaven head, obviously a little thrown by her. She could see the steam rising from the ebony dome of his skull.

'You should get a hat – you wouldn't lose so much heat.'

He nodded. 'Yes, I know.'

This man's nose was beginning to run; he was clearly not made for this country or the weather.

'Rhoda, I'm here about a Mr Maxwell Campbell. I'm Detective Parker.'

He reached into the lining of his coat, put away the notebook and pulled out his badge which he flipped open and presented, a move he had practised on numerous occasions.

'I have a serious matter to discuss with you. Perhaps we could go inside?'

Rhoda stepped aside and let him in, admiring his long gait as he walked down the corridor.

Rhoda's curtains were drawn against the winter sun, which strained through the fabric to cast a comforting, almost womblike haze over the lounge. African masks and framed maps lined the walls that weren't replete with books. Her sofas were covered with vibrant Indian cloths, the corners of the room occupied by wooden fertility carvings. A few stone and bronze characters were displayed on the sideboard. Parker moved towards it and picked up a statue of a man with an elephant's head.

'That's Ganesh. The Hindu god of strength.' Rhoda took the figure from his gloved hands and returned it. 'I'd rather you didn't touch them, they're very old.'

'I'm sorry. I've just never seen anything like that outside a museum.'

'Don't worry. They're better appreciated when viewed without the interference of a piece of glass.' Rhoda stroked its head. 'They're like my babies, different gods from different cultures all representing the same thing. Can I get you a cup of tea or coffee?'

Parker moved towards the maps on the wall. He'd always fancied himself as a bit of a cartographer after finding out as a child that Africa was bigger than North America. Its constant misrepresentation annoyed him. The map was well aged and depicted a very different view to what we know now; for a start it seemed there were only three continents: Africa, Asia and Europe. This looks like an original Ptolemy, Parker thought. That's impossible. Must be a copy.

'I'd love a coffee, thank you.' Parker was still confounded by the map. 'This is truly amazing. It's not real is it?'

Rhoda laughed, 'As if I could afford a real Ptolemic map. No, it's a copy. They're just so fascinating... and educational.' She excused herself to the kitchen and Parker caught himself watching her legs as she left. Not bad, he thought.

He strolled over to the bookshelves. Numerous encyclopedias, ancient history texts, theoretical studies on race, biographies of Malcolm X, Angela Davis, Martin Luther King, Nelson Mandela, Josephine Baker and a mishmash of novels shared a cramped space – Parker was particularly taken by the battered horror novels, especially the dog-eared copies of *Dracula* and *Frankenstein*. He loved horror.

He sat down. The coffee table was covered in old newspapers and letters, he peeked at the closest, trying not to disturb anything. It was only a gas bill.

Rhoda returned and handed Parker his coffee. He took it and held the cup in his hands feeling the warmth slowly work its way through his gloves. Rhoda took the seat next to him; she could still feel the chill of outside seeping off him and dispersing into the room. Sitting so close now he could see her properly. She was striking, the slope of her nose almost European, her eyes slanted slightly, her lips set in a pout from their fullness. You would never find her face boring, constantly discovering new aspects, like the dash of freckles on her cheeks. The musk of her perfume reached his nostrils and aroused his pheromones.

As the story left his lips he studied her reactions but couldn't quite gauge them. He had been thrown by the intensity of her hazel eyes.

'I realise this is hard, but you seem to be the only person we could locate. We just need you to identify him.'

He put his coffee cup down and touched the bare skin of her knee in a gesture of reassurance, secretly wanting to feel her heat.

'This has probably come as a shock. We could leave it but—'

'No, it's fine. It's just the idea of seeing his body.'

Parker removed his hand as she rose from the sofa to prepare for the journey.

'You do understand that he doesn't quite look as you'd expect him to.'

'Yes, yes, I understand—' Rhoda leaned on the armchair as she put on her shoes. 'Where did you say you found him?'

'On a back street. Some local kids thought he was a homeless man resting and ignored him. That is until their dog started chewing on his hand and he showed no resistance.'

Rhoda sat back down. She had visibly paled within the short time he had been in her flat.

'Oh God, I'm sorry.' Parker realised he'd probably gone a little too far, people didn't need to know all the gory details. 'Maybe we should get this over with.'

It was a twenty-minute drive to the station.

Rhoda stared out of the window at the kids loitering on the streets, kicking cans, smoking cigarettes and fighting. Kids always made her pensive. Probably because she knew she'd never have any.

Occasionally she would sneak a glimpse at the detective's hands (now briefly out of their leather binding), they were well taken care of and strong. But it was his skin that really attracted her: it was the richest shade of mahogany she had ever seen. This was something she could definitely get close to.

'Were you seeing each other long?' The resonance of his voice brought her back from her mind's wanderings.

Parker had noticed her looking at him as he had been having difficulty keeping his attention on the road; finding himself compelled to steal glances at Rhoda's bare, caramel-coloured legs, particularly the large white birthmark which appeared with the shift of her skirt every time she leaned forward.

'For a while,' she answered. Parker's car was just as she expected. No trace of any personality. Everything was very clean. The ashtray was unused, the windows smearless, his dashboard dustless, there weren't even crumbs on the floor or seats. The only thing that gave away any presence of a person was the one tape sitting in the deck softly playing Marvin Gaye's 'What's Going On'.

Parker meanwhile was lost in thought. He had never considered himself an envious soul, but from the moment he had seen Rhoda open the door the idea of her possible dead boyfriend lying in the morgue confused him. There was something base about her that aroused hidden instincts he had lost long ago and he was having difficulty ignoring them. Parker had never really had much time for women. His job was his life. But this woman was definitely having some kind of effect on him.

'So it was nothing serious?'

'How did he die?' she asked, avoiding the question, as she leaned forward to turn down the heat in the car. Parker touched her hand to stop her, briefly catching sight of himself in her eyes.

'It's okay, I'll do that.' She turned away and he let go of her hand to switch off the heater. 'A blow to the head. He appears to have been mugged as well. They took his watch and his wallet was empty.'

They walked along sterile and empty corridors, finally arriving at a set of double doors which Parker held open. The intensity of light and the white walls of the morgue hurt her eyes. The smell of chemicals made Rhoda retch, the unnatural acridity masking the unmistakeable odour of death and heightening her unease. The sooner she was out of this place the better. The fluorescent overheads were starting to give her a headache. Somehow it felt inappropriately bright. If the world of Hammer Horror was to be believed, these places were supposed to be dark and crypt-like. Well, she thought, that's progress for you, and put on her sunglasses, receiving a very bemused look from Parker.

'Are you going to be okay with this?' Parker asked, secretly hoping she would faint so he could come to her rescue. They both stood by a sheet-covered corpse. Rhoda nodded. Just hurry up and get the damn thing over with. As Parker pulled back the sheet she saw the pale pink legs and breathed a sigh of relief. Then her gaze travelled up the body reaching his face. She took off her glasses, just to make certain, and then let out a scream.

'But, how can that be?' Rhoda had calmed down and was sitting with Parker at the bar of a nearby drinking hole. 'I know you warned me, but that's impossible. He's a black man but, his skin . . . it was like an albino's.'

'Rhoda, believe me, I'm pretty shocked too.' He sipped his tonic water, trying to drown any further thought on the matter. Much as he enjoyed murder cases this was too bizarre and it unsettled him. How could a black man turn white overnight?

Unfortunately the case was already well known throughout the department, every wannabe detective offering up his opinion or possible solution. Either that or they were looking to him as if he'd have all the answers, just by virtue of melanin. It sickened him, but that was part of survival in the Met. He had to get to the bottom of this or he would never live it down. But there was little he could do until the final pathologist's report arrived tomorrow – then he would have some facts to go on. In the meantime he was determined to find out what, if anything, this woman knew.

'I just don't understand . . .' She stirred her Bloody Mary and tasted it. 'They never put enough Worcestershire sauce in these damn things.' Rhoda pushed the glass away, knocking it over, the rouge of the tomato juice coating the marble bar top and reflecting

Rhoda's pale face. A barman hustled over and wiped up the fallen drink, swiftly replacing it. No charge.

'Thank you for coming with me.'

Parker watched as she put a hand to her unadorned neck and stroked it. I've got to stop looking at this woman, he thought. Remember this is about work. You need to concentrate. Parker moved in his seat, checked the time then looked around trying to ignore the fact she was making him unbearably horny. The place was bog-standard: the obligatory flashy bar and requisite lack of seats too cheaply put together to really pull off the stark modernism it was aiming for.

'He gave me this watch here. For our two-month anniversary. He was a bit of a romantic.'

Parker turned back to her and took the offered hand a little too eagerly. Bending forward to inspect the gold timepiece Parker noticed the patch of white skin on her wrist and almost pulled away instinctively.

'Skin discolouration. It won't harm you. I suffer with it. Have done since I was a child. I use cream but really only the sunshine will help... But I'm not good with the heat.'

Parker nodded, feeling guilty for his overreaction.

The bar was beginning to fill up with the Friday nighters, the hoards of suited workers bellowing and drinking their way into the weekend. In all his years on the force Parker had never partaken in this particular ritual, he was more concerned with getting the job done. His colleagues had invited him down the pub on many occasions but he would always politely refuse, favouring the solitude of his desk and files to an evening of tired stories about police procedures, sexy suspects and stressful domestics. His devotion to work put an enormous strain on the few relationships he'd had. It wasn't that he didn't try, it was just that there wasn't anything interesting enough about any of the women he'd been with to keep him away from his job. Eventually they found someone else to pay them more attention and dumped him.

The two of them had moved to a corner table to avoid the crush that was starting at the bar. Parker tried to entice her into talking about herself, but it was hard work. She kept bringing the conversation round to him.

'So where are your people from? I'm thinking Montserrat,' Rhoda asked.

'Trinidad.'

'Ah, I should have guessed.' She ran her finger along the palm of his gloved hand, pushed up the sleeve of his coat to reveal a sliver of his skin. She touched it. 'You have some Indian in you, too. You can tell by the colouring, a slight touch of chestnut.'

He liked her touching him.

'And you?' he asked.

'Me? I'm a little of everything.' She sat back in her seat and smiled at him, making Parker's stomach churn.

Parker was about to reply when he was shoved forward in his seat by someone passing through the crowd. For once, he didn't react.

Parker hated this kind of place. He hated these booze-fuelled punters. How they lost control and found themselves sharing a stranger's bed or brawling in the street, getting separated by a beat officer. He was glad he didn't have to deal with that any more.

Watching Rhoda slowly lick the stray droplets of the just finished Bloody Mary from her lips, Parker found himself intrigued by the uncanny effect she was having on him. He had heard stories of men being instantly smitten with a woman, some so much so that they lost all control. But he had not experienced anything like this before. Were these those feelings? Parker thought. And if so, what was he going to do about them?

Rhoda lit a cigarette with a shaky hand, the shock, it seemed, had taken its toll. The colour had still not returned to her cheeks.

'Do you ever go off duty?' she said, pointing to his hands. They'd been there an hour and a half and Parker still had his coat and gloves on.

Parker looked down at his clenched fists. He took his gloves off and placed them on the table. Rhoda reached for one and tried it on. The leather was soft, well worn and much loved. They were still warm and a little moist. She rubbed the hide along her arm, then took the glove off and placed it back on the table.

'Did you always want to be a policeman?'

'No, I wanted to live on an island and fish, then at the grand old age of five I was given a panda car. I wanted a real one so... I got one.' He shrugged. 'What about you?'

'Me? I only ever wanted to be dark all over.' Rhoda looked down at the patch on her wrist and rubbed it with the heel of her hand. 'Other than that I wanted to be a nurse,' she laughed. 'But I couldn't stand the sight of blood.'

They carried on talking. Parker probed Rhoda for personal information, but she was a closed book. Every opening he found soon shut in his face; so far he had learnt that she worked as an art dealer and seemed to be of mixed parentage. Parker assumed she was born in London from her accent but couldn't be sure. She was slowly driving him insane.

The two of them sat and watched the customers coming

and going as they waited for the waitress to bring another round. Parker knew that it was not ethical to interrogate a suspect over drinks, especially suspects that were tipsy and on their way to getting drunk, but something deep inside him could not prevent it. Her beauty had blunted his well-honed instincts and her mere presence befuddled his common sense; there seemed to be no other route to cracking through her shell, and he had to discover if she was guilty here and now. He'd known a few detectives who'd sworn by this method, so it was not like he was going to be the first to bend a few rules in order to get the right result. Anyway, Parker had promised himself it would only be the once. After all, he had always believed that old adage about giving someone enough rope. If Rhoda had anything to do with this murder then loosening her tongue and allowing her to talk could ultimately lead to her downfall. Of course if it transpired that she knew nothing then he could take what he was feeling a step further.

'God, look at that woman.'

Rhoda was referring to a blond girl in her late twenties who had obviously made a drastic mistake with her fake tan product. She was the strangest shade of orange, almost luminous.

'I mean do they honestly think that is brown?' She laughed raucously. 'Or that it looks like they've been in the sun? Jesus, why don't they just give up... they'll never have it.'

Rhoda shook her head in disgust. She knew what it was like to want to be really brown... those trips to the salon for a twenty-minute blast in a cancer-can just to turn one shade darker. But why smear your skin with a cream that essentially dyed you? You might as well colour yourself in with a felt-tip pen. Yes, Rhoda could understand why they pursued it. After all, who didn't look better with a tan? What she couldn't stand though was the constant dipping – one week it would be hennaed hands, the next they'd sport a bhindi, the week after they'd be dreading their hair. No one chose to understand the significance; to them it was about fashion, not culture. Didn't they realise what they were doing was tantamount to rape? It didn't take much to pick up a book and learn something.

'Have what?' Parker asked again. She hadn't heard him the first three times.

'It. You know. Please...these people would get jaundice and think they were brown.'

Parker laughed and replied. 'Well, I'm guessing it's their decision. Let them do what they want.'

Rhoda frowned. 'Listen, this skin is important. It protects us.'

'This is our protection?' Parker held up his hand and examined it, turning it over and back. 'Then why does it take someone like me ten years instead of five to reach the position I'm in? You're crazy.'

Rhoda gathered her hair and pulled it round to one side. Parker saw fine blond hairs on the nape of her neck as she bent forward to him. His stomach stirred again.

Rhoda whispered. 'We may have to work harder, granted. But would you want to change the colour of your skin?' She stroked his hand and looked up into his eyes. 'And you know what they say about the darker the berry. You must make women's teeth ache.'

Parker blushed. The last time he had heard something like that was from a girl he'd dated once, a white girl who made him feel like ethnic arm candy. But with Rhoda it was different, coming from her mouth it didn't seem so bad.

Rhoda was now on her fourth Bloody Mary and appeared a little more at ease. Parker had been doing a fine line in staying sober: he still had a job to do.

'Would you not like to talk about what happened to Mr Campbell?'

'I'd rather not think about it, DI Parker.' Rhoda leaned forward and rested her head in her cupped hands. Parker tried to avoid looking down Rhoda's shirt to the swell of her tanned breasts. It was impossible.

'But you must be interested in what happened to him? When did you last see him?'

'How is there an explanation for that? It's like some *djinn*'s taken the soul from him. It's not right.'

'And you last saw him when?'

'A couple of days ago.'

The detective reigned in Parker. 'He's been dead for around three according to the preliminary.'

She leaned back and folded her arms, taking away Parker's viewing material. 'Well then it was three. I don't know... we had an argument and he stormed off in a huff. I didn't know he was going to be killed, did I?'

'Sure, but you'd think you'd remember how long it had been since you saw your boyfriend. I thought women always knew things like that.'

Rhoda sighed deeply. 'Well, I'm not like every woman, detective... Besides, I was going to end it. Me not hearing from him saved me a job.'

Parker continued to push. He had to know if he could discount her as a suspect. As he kept asking questions she flipped out.

'Look, I can't tell you anything. I don't want to talk about it, please. It's too sick,' she shouted, attracting the attention of a group of people close by.

Parker, seemingly embarrassed by the outburst, picked

up his gloves and got up to leave.

'What are you doing?'

Parker stopped.

'Rhoda, you asked me to keep you company and I did. But I think I've outstayed my welcome. I understand that you're upset. Who wouldn't be? I think it would be better if you were alone.'

Parker felt that women were an easy breed to second guess. This one needed him right now and if he threatened abandonment she just might reveal herself to him.

Rhoda grabbed his arm.

'No, stay, please. I'm sorry. Max always said I never knew when to keep my mouth shut.'

He had her now.

That's when Rhoda noticed the Somalian girl. She was just behind Parker, dressed in a black trouser suit, her hair braided close to her skull and covered with a scarlet silk scarf that set off her skin and flawless complexion perfectly. The girl was having difficulty negotiating her way through the sea of people with a handful of drinks; no one relinquishing the little space they had. As she pushed through, Rhoda watched rapt. Parker followed Rhoda's gaze to see the girl spill half her drinks down her suit. Cursing, she gave into the crowd, which promptly swelled around her and carried her through.

'I'll be back in a minute.' Rhoda disappeared into the crowd leaving Parker sniffing the air for a trace of her scent.

Parker's mind raced. Okay so she's asked me to stay. That's good...But her defensiveness when answering my questions? That's not so good...This is all too weird...How can one case and one woman make my head so cloudy? He looked at his watch. Where is she? She can't have been gone long. He sat and waited. The minutes passed. One, two, three, five, ten... Maybe his watch was fast? Maybe she couldn't find the table again through the crowd? Maybe she'd collapsed in the bathroom? Parker stood up and shouldered his way through the throng and headed for the female toilets, stopping before entering. He didn't want to appear too eager, nor did he want her to think that he was checking up on her, that might make her clam up. He decided to stop in at the men's toilet instead.

On making it back to the table Parker found it occupied by a bunch of drunken nine-to-fivers, all presence of her – her coat and her Bloody Mary – was gone. His gloves lay undisturbed amongst the new occupants' drinks. He retrieved them and left.

Sitting in his car Parker looked back over the day. Here was this grandmother of all cases and all he could think about was not the reason for her disappearing but the fact that she had. He forced his detective's mind to spring into action. Could this woman be hiding something? He worked his hands over the steering wheel. He wanted so much to return to where she lived – perhaps it would be worth his while to ask a few more questions, she had avoided most of them all night, and any suspicious behaviour required investigating.

'Oh, it's you.'

Rhoda knew he'd be back.

Parker smiled. She looked different, darker somehow, but that was probably the lack of light in the hallway.

'Come in.'

Rhoda led Parker into the kitchen and pulled out a

seat at the table. Retrieving a glass from the cabinet she poured him a shot of whisky and put it down. She took the seat next to his.

'Why did you come here?' Rhoda crossed her legs. Parker could not help but search for the birthmark; he couldn't find it.

'You look a lot better,' he offered as a response.

'I ate.' She looked down at her lap avoiding his stare.

'I wanted to see if you were all right. You just left. I thought something might have happened to you... You know, a policeman's work is never done.' He downed the whisky and grimaced. Dutch courage.

'I felt queasy and needed to settle my stomach.' She fiddled with the red scarf around her neck.

'That suits you, it complements your eyes.'

'Thank you.' Rhoda looked straight at him. 'Are you hungry, Parker?'

Rhoda switched off the light and the two of them fell into bed. She pulled up his shirt, slid her hand underneath and stroked his back. He kissed her neck and inhaled her fragrance, committing it to memory.

Next door they were used to the noise – the moaning turned them on and perked up their sex life a treat. In fact, much of the time the two of them would lie in bed reading and waiting. But that night it was different, very different, and far more exciting than usual. Instead of the female moaning this was a male voice. He was obviously in the throes of passion as this was the loudest they had ever heard. And as he grew closer to climax he finished with a scream. She must have found herself a new partner, the neighbour thought in mid-thrust. Lucky bastard.

*

Rhoda got out of bed, put on a pair of jeans and a T-shirt, then padded into the kitchen, humming to herself as she put an egg on to fry. Still humming, she went into the lounge and rooted around in Parker's coat pocket. His wallet contained a couple of hundred which she transferred to her jeans. By his coat lay his gloves, she picked them up and stuck them in her back pocket.

Retrieving her travel bag from the hall closet she began to pack the necessities – a few clothes, some underwear. In the lounge she gathered the statues from the sideboard and slipped them into the bag between her clothes for protection. Don't worry guys, you'll be out again soon. She removed the frames from the walls, undid the backs and rolled up the maps, placing them on top of the clothes. She turned to look at her books, she knew all she needed to. Moving again wouldn't be such a bad thing. She could hear the oil spitting, that was fine; everything in its own time.

In the bathroom she gathered her toiletries – toothbrush, toothpaste, Palmer's Cocoa Butter, perm kits, hair dye, wax – and dumped them in her bag. Next she retrieved her trainers from under the sofa, retied the scarf around her neck, grabbed her coat off the rack and put it on. Almost ready now. She walked into the bedroom to kiss Parker goodbye. He looked so peaceful lying there. As she pulled the sheet off him she examined his prostrate body. The once rich hue of his skin was now a pasty white. At least if they ever find you you'll have a smile on your face. She kissed his cheek.

'I hope you enjoyed me, I'll certainly enjoy you.'

Rhoda pulled out his gloves and put them on. They were loose but they felt right. Ready.

Before leaving she took a look in the mirror and touched her gloved hand to her face, her skin now the glossy mahogany of Parker's. She looked radiant. The frying pan caught fire as she walked out into the glorious sunshine, resplendent in her darker shade of brown.

CHAMELEON
Ranbir Sahota

I was white till the age of twenty-four. That was when Mark's mother refused to speak to him. It came as a major shock – as though someone told me I didn't exist, that it was all a lie. I was white in every way, apart from my skin colour – I listened to white music, wore white clothes and ate white food; and I was white enough to marry Mark. I conveniently forgot that I knew how to eat curry with my fingers or clean myself using only my hands and water after a shit; that I spoke fluent Hindi.

My pale face stared back from the bedroom mirror that day. Instead of moisturiser, I applied Fair and Beautiful bleaching cream. Since discovering it in an Indian shop in Southall, I'd rub it into any exposed part of my skin. The tube fell and left its contents smeared over my jeans as the phone rang. Shit. I grabbed for the receiver before my mother did the same downstairs.

'Hello, can I speak to Rita?' squeaked a high-pitched voice.

I grinned, cringing at his poor imitation of a woman,

'Yes, it's me, Mark.'

'Your mobile is switched off again, Rita.' He'd been visiting his parents that weekend and I wondered what could be so important that it couldn't wait till the evening. 'I told my mum about us,' he blurted out.

My heart skipped a beat – wow, I was excited. At last, our relationship was out in the open. What a relief. I smiled.

But Mark seemed agitated and rushed his words. 'If you were from Goa, I could marry you,' he wasn't making any sense. *Goa, but I come from Ealing?* 'She's refused to speak to me if I don't stop seeing you. It's because you're not Catholic.'

'What?' I was confused. 'But I've been to university, I've got a good job and I'm respectable. Maybe I could convert.' Then it hit me. 'It doesn't matter that I'm not a Catholic, does it?'

The phone's crackling seemed very loud and I thought my heart was going to jump out of my chest. 'Rita, I don't think it does, I'm sorry.'

The sound of footsteps on the stairs cut short our conversation. I covered the receiver with my hands and whispered into it, 'I'll be back at the house around six – we can talk about it then.'

For a few moments I sat staring at myself in the mirror. Rita Patel, the Indian, looked back at me. Pretending. Lying. How dare Mark's mother turn me down? Who the fuck did she think she was? She was the daughter of an Irish immigrant. But I suppose she blended in whereas I was an Indian, coloured, even black.

I carried my bag downstairs and smelt the delicious aromas of the Indian foods I'd never learnt to cook. My mother had always been disappointed by my lack of enthusiasm for household skills. The door squeaked as I pushed it open. My father looked up from the television and raised his cup of tea to me in a friendly salute. He would have been far happier in India, I'm convinced of that. He came to England because his friends did and had worked in the same factory for thirty years, never missing a day. I wondered what went on inside his head and imagined him happy, sitting at the water pump on his land in India, surveying his fields with pride. Instead, he had a twenty foot by twenty foot concreted backyard with borders sprouting onions and garlic and a job where he worked all hours for a paltry wage.

There he was – a sitting duck. Someone for me to get pissed off at.

'Dad?'

'Yes, *behta*.' I had his attention.

'Why didn't you just bloody stay in India?'

He raised an eyebrow.

'How many times have I told you not to swear, *behta*?' I sensed his exasperation. Swearing was so unladylike. His mother would have taken a broom to me if she'd heard me. But she was long dead and we weren't in India. 'We came here to work. I wanted to go back but then your mother came and you were born. You know that, I've told you so many times. Now sit down and tell me what you have planned for work this week.'

I didn't want to talk about that. I wanted to talk about why they had given me choices by coming to England. 'If we were in India, I'd be married with children, but instead I'm here and I want more.'

Carefully placing his cup on a table, my father sighed and prepared himself for battle, 'Oh, Rita. Why do you young people have to think you are so mixed up? You can still have all these things. We want you to settle down, have children and a man to look after you.'

'I can look after myself,' I huffed, landing on the shabby sofa, wishing it would swallow me up and spit me out in a whole different world, where everything was simple and white.

My mother appeared from the kitchen scowling at me. She'd heard us through the hanging beads that separated the two rooms. Her sari swished past the china figurine on the coffee table. In her prime, she had been beautiful, truly beautiful. Her long hair had shone in the Indian sun and she was the envy of the village girls. My grandfather had turned away many suitors and settled on my father, as he came from a nearby village, was respectable and had some money, as simple as that. She loved my father and us, but not in the Western way; she was duty-bound.

'Oh, hello Mum. So what do you think I should do to be the perfect daughter?'

She started to polish one of the few remaining ornaments she had brought with her back in the sixties. She only ever polished those, her favourites, leaving the rest of the house to gather layer upon layer of dust. She had lost interest after my sister Seema was born, it had all become too much for her: the home, her job in the sewing factory, us children. 'Come home next weekend and we'll introduce you to some nice fellows, well-educated with good jobs. What more could a woman ask for?'

I smirked and rolled my eyes. It was all so simple for her, she had never had a choice. On her seventeenth birthday, a new sari was laid out on her *munja*. 'Put that on,' her mother had smiled, 'we have guests coming to see you.' By the end of that visit, she had taken her first step to England.

'You children, you never listen to us. You are the eldest, the example.' Her polishing became more furious.

'You are holding the others back and must get married in the next year or so, or no one will want you. If you had let me sort it out a few years ago you would be happy now, with children and a good home and not asking me what to do.'

Normally, I would keep quiet at these moments; it was a mark of respect not to answer back. Good boys and girls only listened and followed their parents' wishes. I could never win these arguments with them anyway, but that day I didn't care.

'Mum, I'm not ready. I'll get married to whoever I want, whenever I want.'

She stopped to stare at me, her polishing forgotten, 'No, Rita, you will not marry whoever, whenever. We will have a say. A decent boy like Mrs Methi's nephew, now he would be perfect.' My mother often tried to push her friends' sons and nephews onto me. It would be ideal, she'd still have a say in my life and I might even end up living close by. Just like the village in India, all the family, all in one place.

I refused to marry Mrs Methi's nephew or anyone else's for that matter and stomped to the door like a spoilt child. That's how they made me feel sometimes, as though I was the one in the wrong. When I was younger, my cousins and I would share tales of girls who agreed to meet a prospective husband and the very same day the reception had been booked. These scare stories only made me want to be with Mark more than ever.

My father joined in, 'Now sit down, *behta*, we only want the best for you. Your future is very important to us. You need an Indian boy from a good family who will respect and look after you, not like those white boys.'

This was going nowhere. My bag was ready by the front door and I headed for it, throwing in a last question out of mischief, 'Dad, but what if I really wanted to marry a white boy?' I always knew this was dangerous territory and wondered if today they would amaze me and say, *behta*, you marry whoever you want to, as long as you're happy. They didn't.

'What, why do you speak of such things? They only want one thing, these white men, they won't stay with you.' My mother's eye was twitching. 'What about all their divorces and infidelities? No daughter of mine will bring a white man into this house!' she bellowed.

We'd had this argument before and every time it was the same. They were so stuck in their ways. They'd come here and wanted it to be just like India. Even over there things had moved on, but they were living in a time warp and wanted to keep me there with them.

In the hall stood my brother and sisters. Seema, my fifteen-year-old baby sister, grabbed my arm and looked distraught, 'Rita, be careful, he was listening.'

My brother Raju pushed her away. He had never liked me. 'Just go, Rita, you're always causing trouble.'

As I turned my car around, I glanced back at the house: my family was staring out from the lounge window, watching me. Instinctively I looked up – Seema was standing alone at the window of my old bedroom. She looked like she was crying.

Mark and I had rented the house in Finchley for two years – no Catholics, no Indians – it was wonderful. The deception was something we had learnt to live with – we only took calls on mobiles and said we worked unusual hours so that our parents never 'just popped in'; if ever a family member did visit though, one of us moved to a friend's. We even had our post sent to work.

Mark was already there that evening and poured some

wine to help me unwind. We'd met at university and he made me laugh like nobody else. He was different from the Indian men I knew, but then marrying an Indian man would have felt like marrying my brother or father, they were all the same. Everything felt so right with Mark. I loved him.

'Don't worry, it'll be all right. There's no way I'm going to let you go. My mother's just crazy, she'll come around.'

I wondered how long we would be able to go on like this. We'd managed two years, so what was another two? I suppose we'd tell them eventually, just not yet. I started crying.

'We don't need them, Rita, we're happy and that's all that matters. My mother can go to hell.'

Mark was so matter of fact. In his world parents could just be brushed under the carpet, pushed out onto the sidelines. But I just kept thinking of what his mother had said. She had always seemed so nice in the photograph on the mantelpiece, now I wanted to smash it to pieces, stamp on it, shout and scream at it; make her change her mind.

She wasn't the only one we needed to talk around. My parents would react the same way, but I expected that. It just seemed so incredible that his parents wouldn't like me. In the past all my white friends' families had welcomed me into their homes, and now I doubted their sincerity. I was fine as the token dark friend but it was a different matter when it came to marriage.

'Your parents are liberal, middle-class people – they're not supposed to be racist. They haven't even met me, and they don't even want to know me. I mean, what did you tell your mother about our future?'

Mark stood up and walked to the window looking out

to the traffic below. He took his time to answer. A cold rush of air blew in from the window and I bowed my head to avoid it. I didn't think my day could get any worse, but it was just about to.

'I told her we'd split up on the phone this afternoon.'

He closed the window and walked over to me. Holding my hand, he said softly, 'Rita, she wouldn't speak to me until I did. It was the easiest thing to do. I'm sorry.'

'Rita, are you really going to marry Mrs Methi's nephew?' Seema seemed upset. 'If he's anything like Mrs Methi he'll be ugly and smell of turmeric.' We both laughed.

'We'll see. Help me pick an outfit.'

We settled on a delicate pink chiffon sari and Seema helped me pin it into place. Now all we had to do was wait. Mum was cooking and we stared out of the bedroom window watching for him. I didn't even know his name.

'Rita,' shouted my mother, 'come and help me tidy, they'll be here soon.'

I put on an old apron and helped Mum set up. My father had gone to Argos that morning and picked up a forty-piece dinner set – it was the first one we'd bought in probably fifteen years. I just hoped it was worth it.

'So how old is this man? Does he earn enough money for me?' I half-laughed and my mother whacked me across the back of my head.

'Don't be so cheeky. You're lucky that we are letting you meet these men. In the old days, you accepted what you were given. Even if he had no money, it was fate, Rita, karma, your destiny. Now you girls think you can dictate what a man should earn – it's disgraceful.'

Ah, I felt a fight coming on. 'Oh, so it's okay for him to expect me to be beautiful, fair and virginal or demand that I live with him and his parents, but I can't hope that he has some cash so that once in a while I can get away from the shit-hole that would be my life.' I'd been reading too many matrimonials in *Des Pardes*, but I hadn't expected what came next.

She swung herself around, stood in front of me and hit her right hand hard across my face. 'Ow, shit, Mum, that hurt!' I wanted to slap her back, tell her to fuck off and stop trying to run my life, but this wasn't the time.

'Just get upstairs and stop screaming like a banshee!'

I stormed upstairs and started to undo my sari. This was such a farce. I was fiddling with the pins when the doorbell rang. Mrs Methi's nephew was waiting to be let in.

Seema rushed in. 'They're here!'

'Let me see. There are three young men down there, which one is Mrs Methi's nephew?' I strained my eyes through the net curtains. One was tall and handsome. The type of guy who probably had a white woman on the side and wouldn't even look twice at me. Another was Sunil Methi, good old Sunil – he was gay, but his parents didn't have a clue. The funny thing was that he could have as many men around to sleep in his room and his folks would be none the wiser. 'Indians aren't gay,' they'd say and change the subject. The other man was small and dark, with what looked like a limp.

They were in: we could hear the 'Hello, welcome, welcome, come in, no keep your shoes on.'

Raju came upstairs to fetch me. Life seemed to have a way of changing so quickly. Last week I was devoted to my white boyfriend and thinking about our future and now I was meeting my prospective Indian husband.

Seema went first and I followed her into the kitchen. My mother twirled me around for a final check, 'Now, this is what you do: don't talk too much, smile, don't look at anyone directly and just serve us. It'll be fine.'

Samosas were laid out on trays and the tea was already in cups. I took a deep breath and walked into the lounge. Everyone stared at me. What would I say to Mark? Was I betraying him? My hands shook a bit as I handed out the tea and put food on our new plates. I caught Sunil's eye and he winked at me.

My father made the most unbelievable introduction ever, 'Here she is. Our beautiful daughter. She's twenty-four with a degree in French. Even though our skin isn't too fair, she has managed a complexion which is the envy of our neighbours. She loves children and is an excellent cook.'

I wondered who he was talking about and blushed. I sneaked a look at the two men and the introductions began. It turned out they were both Mrs Methi's nephews, so which one was I supposed to marry?

'Rita, go into the kitchen and the young man will come on afterwards,' pointed my mother.

The door opened and in came Raju with my suitor following behind. It was the good-looking one. I didn't know if I was relieved or not.

'Hi, I'm Rita,' I offered my hand.

'Sanjay.' He shook it and sat down. 'Auntie called us over because she said you were too good to miss, that you had a good job and a company car. And I hear you speak fluent French.'

He was taking the piss out of me. The cheek of this guy. I liked him – probably only because he was good looking. An ugly guy with the same comments just wouldn't seem so appealing. His hair was cropped close and his eyes were large and very dark.

'You know much more about me than I do about you. My credentials must have impressed you then, you came all this way for my *voiture*.'

'*Mais oui*, I love a woman who speaks fluent French. Do you have a company mobile though?'

'No, it's my own!' We both started to laugh, for no real reason. I fetched a cup for tea, but he went straight for the fridge and found some of Dad's Budweiser. I was tempted to have one myself, but thought better of it. I could imagine the gossip: 'Did you hear about Rita Patel? She got Sanjay Varma drunk and was making lewd suggestions. Young people today are a disgrace.' It wasn't worth it.

'So what's wrong with you? Do you earn seven thousand pounds a year, live with all your immediate family, and want me to lose half a stone in weight?' I'd agreed to this charade but I was damned if I was going to make it easy for anyone. If this was a job interview for my husband then I might as well get down to the nitty-gritty straight away. But really it wasn't that, I wanted to find something wrong with him so I could go back to Mark having tried the Indian way.

'Well, I'm gay for a start and have been having a relationship with my sister for four years.' I shot him a look. 'Only kidding. Nothing's really wrong with me. I stink out the loo sometimes and only go to temple for weddings. I have too many white friends. Mum and Dad seem to think five is quite enough and those should be of the middle-class variety only. But I think the biggest problem may be the fact that I play football with your boyfriend.'

Now this was an eventuality I wasn't prepared for.

'What, what boyfriend?'

'Mark Watts.'

I stared at him, open-mouthed. Best to keep quiet: what if he was a plant? Did my parents know? He continued, 'After a match we all got pissed and he got out your photo and started raving on about you. He told me your name, even said what area you were from. Now how many Rita Patels have a degree in French and look like you?'

I was gobsmacked and wondered what he was going to do. I also felt ashamed that he'd come round for nothing.

'Are you going to tell Mark?'

'No,' he shrugged, 'why should I? None of my business, hey? You can muck him around all you like, nothing to do with me. He seems a nice guy though and there are lots of mixed relationships around, so I don't know why you're doing this shit.'

'This shit? If it's so bad why are you here?'

'Rita, I'm thirty-three. I haven't found anyone my way, so what have I got to lose? I want someone to share my life with. It would be nice to find a girl who will fit in with the family. Someone like you – and I'm not being cheesy now. A girl who can go out drinking with the best of them and visit the temple too. It's not much to ask but I haven't found anyone yet.

'I'm sorry, really I am, but the penny didn't drop until I saw you and they only told me about the French degree on the way here. You know how highly arts degrees are regarded by the olds. They thought it might put me off. Look, you make your excuses— '

For once I was glad to see my mother poking her head around the door. '*Behta*, Mr and Mrs Methi need to leave soon. Finish talking and come in to say goodbye.' We chatted some more and exchanged numbers. I was going to see if I could fix him up with any of my friends. He was nice, and it had been a laugh talking to him, but he wasn't Mark.

After they'd gone, everyone rushed in and wanted to know what had happened in the kitchen. My mother was convinced that we liked each other; after all we'd been in there for a long time. Well nobody had told me that we were only supposed to get to know each other for ten minutes.

'So are you going to marry him then?'

'No, Dad, he doesn't know how to write Hindi. Sorry.'

'Neither do you. Oh, silly girl.'

'And anyway – he's too old.'

I went upstairs to change back out of my sari. My mother stood at the bottom of the stairs, scowling up at me. I ducked into the bedroom, and reached for my phone – it flashed two missed calls from Mark. Even though I wanted to tell him what I was doing, so that he could talk me out of it, or tell his mother to shove it, I ignored them.

Dad, ever the peacemaker, was undeterred.

'No need to worry, we can set up some more meetings for next weekend,' he shouted up.

I didn't say anything, just folded my clothes and lifted my bag downstairs.

I'd seen three other prospectives in the space of six weeks and hadn't got around to telling Mark. Well what did he expect from me? He had denied me to his mother. I needed to see if there was a better way.

She's refused to speak to me if I don't stop seeing you . . . You are holding the others back and must get married in the next year or so.

The words repeated in my head as I woke to see his white skin against mine. I got home the night before around eight after meeting Rajiv, another hopeful. He was nice enough, but he wasn't Mark. What I needed was an Indian Mark. I wondered if one existed.

Placing my hand against his, I noticed that years of Fair and Beautiful had made us almost the same colour.

It was a light tapping at first, tap...tap...tap. The sound of gravel against the window, that's what it was. Mark had always thrown stones at the window to get my attention, but he was lying next to me, so who could be doing it instead? I hoped whoever it was would just go away, but then came the banging on the front door. My eyes were still half closed as I approached the window.

They had seen me. From the corner of our window, I could see the tops of their heads bobbing around, turning from each other to the door and sometimes to where I was standing.

'Oh, my God!' I cried. 'Fuck! Fuck!'

'What?' Mark jolted upright in the bed.

'Rita! Open the door!' cried my mother as my father stood silently behind her surveying our garden. I couldn't believe it, they never visited. They only normally left home for work, shopping, weddings, parties and funerals, but never to visit their daughter.

'Yes, Mum, I'm coming,' I shouted back from the top of the stairs.

The chaos of our room struck me as I turned back to find my dressing gown. Our clothes strewn over the floor, cups, plates everywhere. It was pretty gross, but we hadn't expected a visit that day. Struggling to pull his jeans on, Mark asked what he should do.

'Hide! In the wardrobe!' I ordered.

'You must be joking. This is fucking ridiculous, it's my house, why should I hide?'

'Yeah, like I wouldn't be in there if it was your mum and dad,' I hissed.

They had ruined our day. We'd left the phone off the hook and had planned to laze in bed. Why did they have to show up? I pushed him into the wardrobe which split with a loud crack under his feet.

I laughed, but he didn't. This was going to be really funny to us in years to come. Just not now.

'Ow, I've got a splinter, shit, I think it's a nail,' he winced. Blood was streaming onto the carpet.

I surprised myself – I didn't care too much about his pain. I just heard the knocking getting louder and more urgent.

'Rita . . . Rita Patel open the door, your father needs the toilet,' my mother shouted.

When I finally reached the front door, my mother pushed past me, scowling.

'What took you so long? And for goodness sake put some clothes on, have you no shame?'

I looked down at my bare legs. My father turned his head away and scurried to the toilet.

'Mum, what are you doing here?' I whispered, exhausted.

She was wearing her cooking clothes. She never, ever, went out in her cooking clothes. I was playing out various scenes of hospitals, burning houses, pregnant sisters, but she was surprisingly calm. 'Can't a mother visit her daughter without being questioned?' She shrugged. Almost immediately, she started tidying the lounge, picking up the papers strewn on the sofa, plumping up the cushions. Funny how she'd stopped caring about the appearance of her own home but came to tidy up mine.

I stood in her way. 'Mum, what's going on? Why are you here? I have to go to work soon, you can't stay.'

I hated the way she kept me hanging on, just like years ago, when she'd come back with the shopping and wouldn't let me see. Instead, she'd wait until my brother got home and let him have first choice. He was her favourite, but I was my father's and Raju had never liked that.

She still hadn't explained why they'd come. She was intruding. The house was the one place we could forget about them, and now they were here too. My father came in and just stood there, shuffling with his head down. I pointed to the sofa and finally they sat down. 'We've just come to visit, *behta*, nothing to worry about. Maybe we can talk about a couple of boys we have heard about. I've got some photos,' she smiled.

My head was pounding, but I needed to concentrate. 'I'm going to change,' I fled from the room and as I passed the front door, I was tempted to open it and just walk away.

Mark was crouching in the bottom of the wardrobe with my best blue dress wrapped around his foot to stem the bleeding.

'Listen, I am so sorry. They've just popped round. They want to talk about husbands. I'll get rid of them. I'm so sorry.'

He looked confused. 'Husbands?' I didn't have time to explain and needed to go back downstairs. It was all fucked up.

He grabbed me. 'Rita, this is ridiculous. Let's get it out in the open. Let me meet them. What will they do, kill me?'

I couldn't believe it. 'What the fuck are you talking about? You need to stay here.' I was shaking now.

I needed time to think, but they were downstairs and he was here. Why didn't I just marry Sanjay when I had the chance? If only life were so simple.

Mark was adamant. 'Rita, you'll have to tell them one day, let's make it today. Tell them and I'll tell my mum that it's me and you or she'll have to lose a son.'

I imagined the situation. It was almost comical. My father trying to kill Mark with a kitchen knife and then the screaming as my mother beat me, cursing my lack of gratitude and respect. Would our situation qualify as a news story? How many pages would we get? I could see the headline now: MIXED-RACE LOVERS MURDERED IN NORTH LONDON. Or would we just be another mixed-race love tragedy, old news, done plenty of them before, bring us some mixed-race couples who kill their parents, now that's news.

I didn't want to make a choice and lose either my family or Mark. I wanted them both. I sat on the bed with my head in my hands. I peeked through my fingers and realised it wasn't the dream I had hoped it was. It was real. I didn't know if I wanted to be white any more. At that moment, I wanted to be married to Sanjay, dripping in gold jewellery and pregnant with his child. Now I was paying the price for my wicked Western ways. Yes, I had a bad fate in store, but my parents had come to save me.

'Rita, what are you doing up there?' shouted my mother.

'I'm changing, Mum, I'll be down in a second,' I replied while rushing to the door and locking it.

'I can't do this, Mark. Please don't make me do this.'

Sometimes in daydreams I'd rehearsed the words I would use to tell them. It was always an angry scene. It would destroy what hope they had left of me being the perfect Indian daughter. I'd even written letters many times, but never got as far as putting any of them in an envelope.

'But if we go on like this, we'll spend our lives lying,

hiding – what's the point? Your parents and mine, they're the same. Why do we still need to answer to them? We're not children any more!'

He kept on at me, he was becoming worse than them, but I ignored him. Having a fight with him was the last thing I needed. I dressed quickly and moved towards the door, poking my head out before leaving.

'Mark, I'll get rid of them, please don't come down.'

They were waiting for me. I took a deep breath and tried to strike up a conversation about my brother. My mother didn't bite and continued tidying, looking around with a questioning expression on her face as she caught sight of the empty wine bottle and two glasses.

'Mum, Dad, thanks for coming round, but can we talk about husbands next weekend? I really need to go to work. You know I said to call before popping round as I don't tend to be here a lot.'

'We left messages on your mobile – maybe you could try switching it on sometimes.' Why did I never check that stupid thing?

They exchanged glances and she sat down next to him on the sofa that we'd had such fun haggling for in Camden. I wondered if they'd ever had fun together before we children were born.

'Rita, we haven't come to talk about husbands really.'

The blood rushed to my cheeks and I avoided their gaze by busying myself with sorting through our magazine collection. How could they know? We had been so careful.

They looked at each other, and my father nodded for her to speak. 'You know the Methis have been our oldest friends. Well, they have a major problem. It's like this— ' why didn't she just get on with it? '—Mrs Methi's daughter has run off with a white man.' She looked at my father as though she were in pain. 'Her parents are beside themselves with grief. You used to go to school with her, didn't you? Mrs Methi wanted me to help find her, so please Rita, tell me what you know.'

I relaxed and tried not to show my relief, it was Meena Methi and not me they wanted to focus on. Meena had always been the quiet one at school, reading her romantic novels in the corner. Her parents were strict, they didn't even let her cut her hair. I couldn't believe she'd run off with a white man. 'I haven't seen Meena for a long time,' and that was the truth.

'Can I get you a drink before you go?' I offered as I headed towards the kitchen, kicking Mark's shoes under the sofa along the way.

I looked around searching for hints of Mark. Nothing in the kitchen. That surprised me as he did most of the cooking, not like my father. He'd had to learn, though, when he first came to England, otherwise he'd have eaten fish and chips and no *roti* for three years. But after my mother came, he never cooked again, he'd have rather stayed hungry than prepare food – that was women's work.

The door slowly opened behind me and my father slid into the kitchen. He looked anxious and kept glancing around. I think she had sent him in; he'd always got the truth out of me when I was a child.

'Rita, it's a terrible thing about Meena, isn't it? The Methis are like family, we need to help them. Girls like that are left with fatherless children without an identity. I don't know how she could do that to her parents,' he whispered. 'Are you sure you don't know where she is? Her parents only want to talk to her, stop her from ruining her life.'

My mother was quite settled on our sofa and determined to return to the Methis' misfortune.

'Meena met this man at university, you know? We heard he was already married and is much older than her. What a stupid girl. We know you'd never do anything like that.' She chose her words carefully while my father remained silent throughout.

'No, Mum, don't be silly. Listen, I really need to get ready for work.'

But she didn't want to stop. Mum just kept on repeating the same thing. She was trying to drum her beliefs into me, to brainwash me, making me feel like Meena's crime was my crime.

I'd had enough, they would never change.

Tapping on our bedroom door, I whispered for Mark to let me in. I was glad to see that he'd managed to stem the bleeding.

'Are you okay?' we asked each other simultaneously.

I locked the door behind me and we lay on the bed together staring at the ceiling.

There was something nagging me. Why didn't they call me? Why the visit? Oh yes, my bloody mobile was switched off. But it wasn't that, it was Meena who was bothering me. This whole search party thing wasn't the Methis' style. They'd keep it quiet and not shout it from the rooftops, especially with my mother leading the troops.

I got up and started rummaging through my bag, searching for my address book. P, R, S, there, Sunil Methi. He picked up quickly. I was cautious at first, not wanting to waste his time, he could be waiting for a call from her.

'Hi, Sunil, it's Rita, I hope you're okay.' I really hated

to intrude, and held my finger to my mouth as Mark looked up at me puzzled.

His voice seemed fine, bright in fact and he didn't mention Meena at all, so finally I did. I hoped he didn't get too upset.

'Oh, you heard. She's up north somewhere, I reckon. You know she went to uni in Leeds, probably staying with a mate up there. My parents are really stressed out. Good luck to her is what I say.' Sunil had always supported his elder sister. 'But you must be in the same situation. I met Raju yesterday. How did your folks' visit go?'

'What visit?'

'Oh, didn't he tell you? Raju said that they were sick of introducing you to guys while you were still with Mark and were coming to have it out with you.'

That bastard Raju. He had told them.

I made an excuse and hung up. They were here for me all along.

I lay back down on the bed and just shook my head at Mark. I would explain later. It was just so peaceful there as the breeze from the window cooled me down. I turned to him and smiled.

Downstairs, I opened the door. 'Mum, Dad, I'd like you to meet someone.'

THE BEGINNING

Diana Evans

At the junction between Neasden Lane and Church Road, North-west London, there is a grass-topped roundabout lined by a row of shops. A grocer smelling of cumin. A newsagent that doubles as a post office on Wednesday afternoons. A betting shop. A workmen's café whose most celebrated dish is apple pie, destaled by steaming lumps of ageing custard.

Along this terrace Bessi walks with Dad and Gracie to where the funeral parlour meets the big, wide road – the end of the world. The sun has turned itself inside out so that she burns white instead of gold, a ghostly incandescence drifting through flocks of cloud. Bessi keeps tripping over her boots, looking down at the ground as if convinced it could disappear a little more with each step she takes. At her arm is Gracie, holding onto Bessi's elbow and to her obligations as a big sister with an unstinting dedication. Dad clenches his red fists intermittently and grips winter in his puffing cheeks. He waddles on behind his belly, which leads the way; a great bulbous nose navigating its fumbling herd towards a destination they still only partly believe is theirs. The End. In their startled eyes, moments and meanings have been irreversibly altered and new and darker shadows shift and shroud. Their lashes tremble. They look as if the wind could knock them down.

But Bessi, there is a smile behind her lips where she's kissing me.

JPW Funeral Directors looms in gold-plated glory above itself, the huge lettering swallowing up the shaded window front with its plastic flowers statued next to the front door. It looks quieter, private, more still than the other buildings, the silence of death burning through concrete. It sits at the end of this grubby row of shops like a displaced punctuation mark, wishing it could be somewhere else, somewhere less public and less stained with the everyday; some sweet-smelling, belch-free suburban cul-de-sac where discretion was absolute. To this delicate ideal, across the breadth and length of the glass door, a slender black cross pays tribute. Elegant and shining from fresh Windolene, it stops the bewildered party like a final sigh, as if it were the end itself; the very gates to heaven, both gentle and foreboding. The three of them stand watching the door, leaning towards it with their bodies, lurching away from it with their hearts.

'There's still a few minutes yet,' Dad fiddles with his watch and looks around at the others, 'we're early... if you're not ready yet.'

'No, let's just go in. There's no point in waiting out here,' says Grace. 'Bessi, you ready?'

She nods and Dad knocks on the door.

A puny man in grey tweed and a crimson bow tie, his face half-hidden behind a fat moustache, pulls it wide open and Bessi shudders. It's cold in there. It's cold and dark and full of coffins and corpses. Yet the man, I've named him JP, smiles richly beneath the moustache, pink flooding his cheeks, and welcomes them inside to a blast of unexpected, electric heat. They step into a dim hallway whose walls give off that same quality of unearthly stillness.

'Mr Hunter. Hello. I'm Jonathan Pole.' Dad shakes JP's hand and they both beam pinkly. Dad has a beam for every situation. Here it's solid, sentimental, somewhat pinched, but definitely a beam, with his grey eyes dancing sadly behind his glasses.

'This is Bessi, Georgia's twin. And Grace, her older sister.'

Gracie lets the same flat beam spread across her face despite her usual sturdiness of character, while Bessi raises her eyes to JP's. He looks kind and we like him. There's a sensitive humour that hums around his fluffy grey hair, as if he has gradually come to use it as a quirky demeanour to deal with the business of administrating death. The pale, lifeless bodies unloaded into his basement before funerals, the weeping relatives timidly knocking at his door, the coffins and memorial stones groaning within his catalogues. He looks back brightly into Bessi's eyes and shakes her hand as if he were greeting a child. Won't you come through, and he leads them into his shiny mahogany office, Bessi looking around at the dark-olive leather-bound chairs and the pictures on the wall of North-west London historics, trying to choke back the strange laughter welling in her throat. This elegiac cubbyhole, with its respectful tranquillity and old-fashioned luxury, is the darkest place on earth yet it seems to rock with some titanic, immortal joke made up of all the tears and the whimpers of its clients past and present, a kind of retaliation against an existence devoted to misery.

Bessi nudges me in the stomach with her muscles because Dad wouldn't understand. Unlike JP, he is not well versed in the comedy of post-purgatory telepathy, or the divine inhabitations of spirits. He'd think Bessi was losing her mind. After all, there's nothing funny about arranging your daughter's funeral, deciding the exact fashion in which to lay her defunct flesh to rest. What type of service, which site for a grave, how many flowers. Yellow. She loved yellow.

'Won't you please take a seat,' and we ease ourselves down. Straight-backed. Dutifully melancholic. Perched for dreaded discussion.

'Murray Mint?' JP offers warmly.

'Um, well, yes, why not?' Dad accepts and Grace refuses. Bemused, Bessi chokes silently and takes a sweet, the wrapper fizzling in the quiet air as she twists it open.

'Can't go wrong with a Murray,' I spurt through Bessi's lips and Dad snaps a haunted look her way.

For an instant, in a certain swing of light, his eyes catch mine. He squints and leans towards Bessi checking for any grotesque supernatural miracles that may have passed him by, then leans back again, succumbing to confusion and the cruelty of memory. He always had difficulty telling us apart – why should it be different now?

Bessi sucks loudly on her sweet, shuffling deeper into the rocking chair sucking on her, swallowing up her tiny frame. JP flicks his eyes around at his guests, judging for tact and timing, and takes the sucking, fidgeting silence for readiness.

'Now,' he says, 'you've been to see her, to identify the body?'

'Yes,' replies Grace, 'we just came from there.'

'And I shall assume it's her...'

'Yes, it's her... in a way.'

'Hmm, I understand, it's very strange seeing the body of a loved one. Never quite seems like them.' JP rests his gaze on Bessi. 'Pretty thing she must have been. Were you identical?'

'Yes.' Bessi's chair squeaks. 'We are.'

'And so young... my sincere condolences to all of you.'

'Thank you,' Dad responds. 'It has been a real shock.'

JP lets the acknowledgement settle before moving on.

'Right,' he says, leaning towards the three huddled together around the desk. 'This is a very sensitive matter and it helps to be as frank as possible.'

He gives them another moment to collect themselves and prepare for a deepening of morbidity.

'Of course,' Dad asserts again, forever cooperative.

'Are you thinking of cremation or burial?'

Dad looks at Bessi for the answer. They've discussed it already and decided that burial is best because Mum doesn't believe in burning bodies. Despite Bessi telling them that she knows for sure that I'd want my ashes to be whirled and swirled around the flowers on the Sussex Downs, where me and Gideon used to make love swathed in golden rays, to dance and float with the breeze until they sank into the earth and grew inside the new stems, becoming alive all over again, with brand new colours.

'Burial,' she says.

Mum knows best. Mum hurts most. And at least they will have somewhere to think of me, to eat banana and peanut butter sandwiches and talk to me with the slight embarrassment and shiftiness of those who talk out loud to the dead.

'Burial,' Dad confirms with a gloomy nod.

JP strokes his tweed cuff before moving on. 'Yes, right. Well, most of our clients use the Kensal Rise Cemetery.'

We know it. Skipped along that old and dusty sky-scraping wall that runs from the flower shop in Harlesden to the Sunday flower stall at Ladbroke Grove when we were kids, always wanting to jump over and see the transparent ghosts wandering through the stones. I know now the ghosts don't really exist. Not white and murky like the fake photos make out. We are lace shining around the living who still need us, like Bessi needs me; reflecting their thoughts, holding her arm through the rainy streets, counteracting her loneliness for as long as she believes I am there.

' . . . and, of course,' continues JP, 'you could have a double grave . . . perhaps . . . for her twin?'

Bessi's eyes widen. 'How does that work?' She stops just short of using JP's recently acquired nickname.

'As it sounds, my dear,' he replies, a knowing smile pushing past his lips. 'A single grave is deep enough for one person. A double is dug twice as deep. So, for example, Georgia would be buried, and when you follow, you would be buried above her. With space left on the inscription for your name.'

Space left for my name. For Bessi the thought is like the promise of a painless death.

Dad looks round at her and this time they beam in unison. 'Oh, yes, yes, that would be wonderful,' she says. She's thinking of her decaying bones joining the same soil as mine, her body suspended within the thick, wet earth; and my own belated body, her foundation. It is a bizarre privilege to know the exact plot of land that will cushion her coffin, to walk through life with an image of where it ends. Next year, in fifty years, tomorrow. She could die right now and jump gleefully into the ground, inscribe her own name next to mine and join me, laughing and swimming in all this limitless, rolling space that now is just a flutter at her breath and beneath her walking.

'Fine,' says JP. 'This option usually provides some relief, however insignificant it may seem in the long run.'

'Yes, it's a lovely thought,' Grace affirms.

JP moves on swiftly.

'Now, coffins. We've got coffins and caskets in oak and mahogany. A variety of finishes and linings.'

He gathers some loose sheets of card from his desk showing photographs of coffins suspended on a white background. Each has a blurb beneath describing the model's particular credentials of wood and decoration and economics. Bessi, Grace and Dad lean forward and crane their necks to try and see which one to choose, none of them really knowing what they are looking for. A coffin is nothing more, nothing less. Tragic. Sordid. Haunting. Not subject to preferences of style or texture or colour. They sweep their eyes over the woods, reading nothing, perplexed.

JP senses their difficulty and offers, 'Many people find it almost impossible to choose like this. Perhaps you'd like to view a few now?'

'Now? Where now?' Grace looks confused.

'We have a collection upstairs.'

'Oh, right, of course... silly me... but how *weird!*'

The image scoots across Bessi's mind and the others seem to be able to see it too: coffins, rows and rows of them, stacked up like biscuits in Tesco. Categorised according to toppings and centres, brands and price tags. Coffins with bar codes. She wants to tell JP that we did not come here to shop but also agrees with me that it would be inappropriate. Instead she seconds Grace's exclamation with a hearty nod.

'Weird!'

JP seems used to the response. He rises like a hermit and an outcast proud of his turf and its power to evoke wonder. 'Follow me,' he says with a new bass in his voice.

We climb the stairs after him to a room at the top dwarfed by mammoth shelves of all-sorted coffins. It's a little more selective than the Tesco version – display goods rather than actual merchandise – and there's less aisle space. Squashed into the little gap left for him in which to conduct his showcase, JP shoves a weedy forearm into the white, linen lining of a glorious sand-hued six-footer, the silence of the empty caskets giving way to the sound of leaves trembling at the icy window.

'The veneered oak is a popular choice for the younger ones... Mahogany's generally more mature, as are the caskets. People say its colour is too heavy... something like that.'

Dad wipes water from his eyes. He takes off his glasses and pretends they need cleaning, bowing his head in feigned concentration as JP proudly moves on to a scarlet velvet-covered casket on the top shelf, his arm raised and outstretched in a gesture of fond salute to his most prized model.

'And here, the Garratt Casket. Solid oak. A soft, velvet cover. This one we call the ripe cherry but we have other colours – purple, gold and emerald green.'

It's grotesque. A monster of a thing and I'm not going *anywhere* in that.

'It also comes lined with taffeta. As, of course, do all the others, come lined, I mean. Nice if you're wanting an open casket...'

I give Bessi a nudge in the ribs and she quickly says yes, Gracie and Dad affirming with bewildered nods. This is melodrama, this is masquerade. I want them to see me in my flowered dress all spruced up to meet the earth. I want my lashes stroked along to the tops of my cheeks, my face ruddy with these last few days of human visibility. I want Gideon to place a tomato, a final tomato, next to my waist, just like he did when we met, as they lay me down in the five-foot-five, feather-cushioned pine, that one, that one there, with the varnished curls carved on each side...

'Georgia says she wants this one.' Bessi squeezes over to the smallest coffin in the room, by the window, and runs her hand along its curly detail.

...I want drums and soaring voices rattling in the sun-shocked wind as I go lower and lower. No tears, no howling, Mum, just the joy, the relief, the laughter. And then the peace cascading down as I fall.

Gracie's eyes are glazed as she looks at her sister. 'If you say she wants that one, Bessi, let's take that one.' My twin has accepted her role as intermediary between the before and after with impressive skill and discretion.

'Good choice I say,' JP enthuses, casting a quick, longing glimpse at his beloved Garratt as he leads his customers back downstairs.

'Now, the coroners will be bringing her down on Friday. So if you could come back then and bring her clothes with you, something, perhaps, that she particularly liked, you understand, then she'll be ready on Tuesday for the service.'

A flowered dress of ruby and shaded leaves waits for me one last time. At home, in the pastel-polished flat I called home, she sits amongst the other cold garments, waiting for Bessi to find her.

'We have to do the make-up as well, so if you could bring that too...' JP continues.

'Oh, I'll do her make-up.' Bessi reads my mind. She's

wary, I am wary, of white males doing make-overs on black skin already dusted with death. JP's bound to get the foundation wrong.

'Yes, of course. Right you are. That's *fine*, fine,' he beams at Bessi and turns to Dad. 'We'll just straighten out the particulars now, Mr Hunter, and then I'll see you back here on Friday.'

Yes, JP, we'll be back with the right make-up and my clothes, and Gideon's final tomato. Take care, now, how you handle my body. I've heard horrid stories about funeral parlours and their sick staff, shoving bodies around like they were old bits of rubber. No respect. Handle me like I was a rose petal floating on a lake. Softly, slowly, tenderly; spruce me up nice and I will remember you. Bessi, shall we?

BIOGRAPHICAL NOTES

Jamika Ajalon has performed her gritty, visceral, lyrical poetry at venues in the US, the UK, France and Africa, with the Urban Poets, the Tony Allen Band, the Shrine and too many DJs to mention. She frequently tours France with Zenzile and lyricises her poems on albums *Zenzile Meets Jamika 5 + 1*, *Sound Patrol*, and features on Eva Gardner's compilation *aphrodisia 3*. She's appeared solo at many London venues, among them the Scala, the Jazz Cafe, the Fridge, the Barbican, the Spitz, the Foundry, LIFT, NITRObeat, the ICA and the Queen Elizabeth Hall.

She's had poems published in *Gargoyle*, *Wasafiri* and the collection *Bittersweet: Contemporary Black Women's Poetry*, ed. Karen McCarthy. A short story, 'Kaleidoscope', was published in *Afrekete: An Anthology of Black Women Writers*, ed. Catherine E. McKinley and L. Joyce DeLaney and in *Sappho Küsst die Welt*, ed. Kathë H. Fleckenstein. Her journalism has appeared in the *Black Book Review* (NY), *Outlines* (Chicago), the *BFI Black Film Bulletin*, *Black Filmmaker*, the *Voice* and *Straight No*

Chaser. Jamika is writing her first novel.

Malaysian-born writer **Francesca Beard** is based in London. She started performing poetry five years ago and has rapidly established herself as an artist with a far-reaching future, as recognised by London Arts, who recently awarded her funds to develop a one-woman show. In April 2002, she represented British poetry at Torino, for the Biennale Internazionale Arte Giovane. The *Independent* has described her work as 'spine tingling' and the *Evening Standard* called it 'utterly magical'. She has performed at many international festivals including Roskilde, Denmark, the Edinburgh Fringe, Glastonbury and Hay-on-Wye and at many major venues including London's Royal Festival Hall and the ICA. Her work has appeared in *Dazed and Confused*, *The Idler* and *Oral* (Faber & Faber Centenary Collection). Her chapbook of thirty poems is now in its fourth reprint. She has appeared widely on national television and radio. She is co-founder of the art-house band 'Charley Marlowe'.

Donna Daley-Clarke is British and lives in London. Her parents are from the Eastern Caribbean island of Montserrat. She graduated in October 2001 from the Creative Writing MA at the University of East Anglia. Her work has been anthologised, most recently in *Her Majesty* (Tindale Street Press, 2002). She is currently working on her first novel, *A Lazy Eye*.

Krishna Dutta was born and brought up in Calcutta and has been living and working in London as a teacher for over thirty years. She has co-authored with Andrew Robinson several books on Rabindranath Tagore, published in the UK, US and India, including an anthology of translations of Bengali short stories, *Noon in Calcutta*, published by Bloomsbury. She is currently writing a book on Calcutta. This is her first short story.

Diana Evans started her writing career as the arts and music editor for *Pride* magazine. She went on to publish literary criticism, dance and music coverage and human interest features in the *Independent*, *Marie Claire*, *The Stage*, *Source*, NME.com and other titles. Her interviews have included Maya Angelou, Mariah Carey, Alice Walker and Lauryn Hill. She has also been a *Calabash* editor and lectured in feature writing. Her creative writing is published by *Poetry Today*, *Wasafiri* and *IC3: The Penguin Book of New Black Writing in Britain* (Penguin, 2000). In 2001 she was awarded a residency at Hedgebrook Writer's Retreat in the USA, where she continued work on a novel-in-progress. She is of Nigerian and English parentage and lives in London.

Barbara A. Graham, 40, is of Jamaican descent and was born and raised in East London. She is the mother of three teenagers. Her love of writing has evolved from journaling after the death of her father. She currently works in Education at Newham Sixth-Form College and is studying for an English degree part-time at North London University. She has been a member of the Sable creative-writing group and also studied with Leonie Ross at the City Lit adult education centre.

Amanthi Harris was born in 1970 in Colombo, Sri Lanka, and moved to the UK in 1980. She attended Bristol University and has degrees in Chemistry and Law. She has worked as a solicitor, an editor, a bookseller and temped while writing her first novel.

Heather Imani was born in London to Jamaican parents. Her work has been published in two anthologies: *Playing Sidney Poitier and Other Stories* (ed. Catherine Johnson, Saks Media Publications, 1999) and *IC3: The Penguin Book of New Black Writing in Britain* (ed. Kadija Sesay and Courttia Newland, Penguin, 2000). Though she writes mainly prose and poetry, Heather has recently started writing for the stage and screen. Her ten-minute screenplay, adapted from her published short story 'Elenah's Telling', gained her a place on the MA screenwriting course at the Northern Film School at Leeds Metropolitan University, where she is currently studying.

Sharon Jennings is an African American who grew up in Los Angeles and has lived in Britain since the mid-1970s. She currently works as a training and management consultant, is a lecturer in social care for the Open University and is the mother of three teenage daughters. She has written articles and publications on race and mental health issues and is now focusing on writing fiction.

Kalbinder Kaur is a 24-year-old writer, born and raised in Stoke-on-Trent. Her parents migrated from Punjab India in the early 1970s; her mum works in a factory and her dad is a taxi driver. She graduated in sociology from the University of Warwick, where she won its Short Fiction Prize in 2000. She has spent the last year in Oxford, where she was an outreach worker for an Asian women's project. She also set up the creative writing group, Random Writers, there. She is currently working on her first novel and has just joined an artists' colony near

Madras for six months.

Shiromi Pinto has worked as a freelance arts writer and editor. Her first short story, 'Bulat Kisses', was published in Canada (where she grew up) in 1995, and was awarded second prize by the publisher as part of its annual short story competition. A more recent work, 'Kolambe', a travel memoir appeared in the autumn 2001 issue of the *Toronto Review of Contemporary Writing Abroad*. Shiromi is currently a writer and editor for the Commission for Racial Equality. She lives in East London.

Born in Leamington Spa, **Ranbir Sahota** is the daughter of Indian Sikh parents who came to England in the 1960s. She is the youngest of three children and now lives with her husband and son in South-east London.

Ranbir took what was considered an unconventional route to higher education for Indian teenagers in the late 1980s, and studied arts subjects for A Levels and German and Russian at Sheffield University. After university, Ranbir taught English in Hamburg for a year and then settled in Manchester to study further and start working in public relations. After six years, Ranbir decided to give up the world of work and instead travel around Southeast Asia, Australasia, the South Pacific and India with her husband. While abroad, she qualified as a Dive Master and worked in Vanuatu in the South Pacific guiding divers to depths of 60 metres around the largest accessible ship wreck in the world. While travelling, Ranbir negotiated the publication of an article chronicling her travels for the *Manchester Evening News*.

Nicola Sinclair was born in September 1974 and raised in North-west London by a Guyanese mother and a

British father. A huge fan of horror and science fiction, she works as publicity manager for Gollancz where she spends her time touting the merits of these largely ignored genres to the unconvinced literati. She believes that genre fiction is an area of writing where the true intellectuals of the world explore their deepest thoughts about society, politics and even race, but are routinely ignored because people think they are all going to be about men and their spaceships. One of her favourite books is Richard Matheson's vampire story *I Am Legend*, and she also believes that everyone should read at least one Philip K. Dick or Octavia E. Butler novel before they die.

Saradha Soobrayen was born in North London in 1974 and grew up in Tottenham. She is currently based in Barnet, Hertfordshire, and spends time at the family home in Mauritius. She studied at Manchester Metropolitan University, and received a BA (Hons) Degree in Creative Arts, specialising in Writing, Visual Arts and Live Arts. She has worked alongside other writers, poets and artists and has given readings of her work at various venues in London. She currently spends her time doing voluntary work for the national charity Lupus UK and is working on a series of short stories and her first collection of poetry.

Gemma Weekes graduated from Brunel University in 2000, studying English with Film & TV. She is a poet, singer, songwriter and freelance journalist currently working on her first novel. She was published in *IC3: The Penguin Book of New Black Writing in Britain* (Penguin, 2000), and has performed at various venues around London including the Royal Festival Hall, Farrago 'Slam',

Urban Griots, Jamaica Blue, the Newham Millennium Festival, the Black Women Mean Business Valentine's Day Reception, the Jazz Cafe, Soul Food and the Bug Bar. She currently lives on a sofa in East London and dreams of a life without daily body-popping to sort her back out.